Different Lives

2 novellas in one volume

Doppelganger

and

Flipside

By Jenny Twist

"There is a fifth dimension, beyond that which is known to man. It is a dimension as vast as space and as timeless as infinity. It is the middle ground between light and shadow, between science and superstition."
Rod Serling

Contents

Doppelganger

By Jenny Twist

This is a work of fiction. Any resemblance to the living or dead is entirely coincidental.

Credits

Editor: Emily Eva Editing
http://emilyevaediting.weebly.com/

Cover Art: Caroline Andrus
http://candrus-designs.com

This story was originally published by
Mélange Books, LLC
White Bear Lake, MN 55110
www.melange-books.com

All rights have now reverted to the author.

Dedication

For Simon Fenwick

Doppelganger, Double-ganger, of G. *Doppelganger*. The apparition of a living person; a double, a wraith.

Doppelganger

Christine lay in the bath sipping a glass of wine and staring at her toes. She had quite nice feet, she thought. A little chubby, perhaps, but a pleasing shape, the toes even and straight. In fact, she wasn't bad looking altogether. Despite bearing two children she retained a shapely figure. She had stretch marks, of course, fading to silver now, and scarcely noticeable, and her breasts were perhaps on the large side. Kevin thought so, anyway. He laughed at her bra on the line, saying it looked like a couple of potato sacks. And she used to think he was such a kind and loving person.

She scooped up a handful of pills and knocked them back with another sip of wine. It was taking much longer than she had expected. She'd had to run more hot water in twice and had to get out to get another bottle of wine and more pills. She'd used all the painkillers she could find—paracetamols, aspirin, ibuprofen, even the children's junior aspirin and was now starting on the rest of the stuff in the bathroom cabinet – antihistamine, diazepam, something for diarrhoea. They all said not to exceed the stated dose, which just goes to show how much leeway there was.

She had considered slashing her wrists, even gone as far as bringing the sharp kitchen knife into the bath, but she couldn't bring herself to do it. An overdose seemed so much more civilized, less messy. And if you did it in the bath, you'd slide under the water when you passed out and there would be no question of botching it.

Except she wasn't passing out.

She scooped up another handful of pills. She was wearing a swimming costume. Even though she would be dead when they found her she couldn't bear the thought of being found naked. "Over my dead body," she thought, and gave a hollow laugh.

She had planned this quite meticulously. Kevin was away for the weekend. With a poetry workshop, he said. Ha! She would have believed him once.

The children were at her mother's for a few days. Her mother didn't know. Nobody knew. Except Kevin, of course.

It was all so bloody unfair. She had tried so hard. He, being a poet, couldn't be expected to work and support a family. And so she was the one who had worked full-time, been the bread-winner, brought up the children single-handedly and done all the housework.

He hadn't wanted children. Didn't want the responsibility. But it wasn't just that. She took another sip of wine. He wanted all her attention. The children were rivals for her affection.

God, this wine was disgusting! It seemed a shame, when it was the last thing she was ever going to drink. But it was all they had in the house. Two bottles of Bulls Blood, which she had already drunk, and a couple of bottles somebody had brought to a party that had never been opened. She squinted at the label. Concorde British Red Sparkling Wine. Well, that said it all really, didn't it? The other bottle was some kind of liqueur, or possibly spirit − Old Vic. It looked like a urine sample. Probably both bottles had been to several parties before they ended up at the back of her kitchen cupboard.

She had left a note explaining how she felt. She'd told him already, of course, but he hadn't taken her seriously. "For God's sake, Christine," he'd said, "Pull yourself together. Everyone does it. It doesn't mean anything." And when she had protested that you were supposed to be faithful, he had laughed. "Do you know a single couple where one of them hasn't had an affair? Name one."

And she couldn't. Can you believe that? Every couple she knew one of them had had a fling at some point, usually the man.

It was just that she had thought they were different, she and Kevin. She had thought they were happy.

"Don't pull that holier than thou act with me. You're out every night till all hours."

She had gasped, so shocked she couldn't speak for a moment. "You don't think I've been unfaithful, surely?"

And he had turned away with a weary expression. "Come on, Christine."

"Kevin." She grabbed him by the arm and made him face her. "When have I had time to have an affair? I'm out all night because I'm on night shift at the factory. And anyway," she said, adding the clinching argument, "all my underwear is grey with baggy elastic."

He had looked back at her completely uncomprehending. He was so convinced that the whole world, including her, had sex whenever and with whomever they fancied that he couldn't believe that she had not. He was so adamant that she began to doubt her own memory. Maybe she had had affairs and somehow forgotten about them.

She looked at her feet again. They seemed to be getting further away. Could she be *stretching*? She sloshed the last of the Concorde British Red Sparkling Wine into the glass and scooped up some more pills. Some of them fell off the table and rolled across the floor.

"Fuck!"

She never used to swear. Her friends laughed at her because she would shout things like, "You naughty boy!" at drivers who cut in front of her. But years of living with children made you watch your language. The last few weeks she hadn't cared. Had sworn on purpose, in fact. Trying to shock Kevin. Trying to make him understand how hurt she was. It did no good. He just walked out of the house and went off by himself. To meet Daphne. *Daphne,* for God's sake! What kind of a name was that? What could her parents have been thinking of? Although maybe it was appropriate. Wasn't Daphne a nymph?

She was little and thin, with no tits to speak of, like a child. It was incredible to her that Kevin could want to sleep with her. It was like paedophilia. And besides, it was insulting. Daphne had nothing about her – no personality, no intelligence. Kevin said she was his muse. You'd think a muse ought to at least be able to do joined-up thinking.

Perhaps if she had taken more care of herself. Not had children. Stayed slim . . . she knocked back the last of the wine.

"Fuck," she said, eyeing the empty bottle with disgust. You really would have thought three whole bottles would have been enough. There was nothing else for it. She was desperate. She was going to have to drink the Old Vic. She grabbed the sides of the bath and tried to sit up. None of her limbs were prepared to cooperate. Her arms turned to jelly and her legs buckled under her. Slowly and with something like gratitude, she slid under the water.

If she had just been slimmer . . .

~*~

She woke up in a white room − white ceiling, white curtains. She was lying on a huge bed covered in a white bedspread made of some silky material. She stretched her arms out to her sides. The sheets were silk as well. The bedspread had a subtle pattern of very pale pink rosebuds. They appeared to be embroidered by hand. Exquisite!

The room was very big. She could practically have fitted her whole house in it. And there was very little furniture. Besides the bed itself, there was a low coffee table in some kind of blond wood, two small easy chairs, upholstered in the same white silk with rosebuds, and a cheval mirror in the same blond wood as the coffee table. She looked around. The bed head was also in blond wood, as were the fitted shelves and bedside tables on either side.

On the wall beside her was a row of switches. She reached over and pressed the nearest one. A light came on over the bed, discreetly angled to rest on her pillow, but not to impose on the other side. The next switch operated the overhead lights. She looked up to see a row of heavy chandeliers. Amazing!

The third switch didn't immediately seem to do anything. Then she became aware of a faint swishing noise and realised the curtains at the other side of the room were sliding open. She gasped. Beyond the window was a vast expanse of turquoise water and pale blue sky.

She swung her legs out of bed, about to go over and get a better look, and was arrested in mid-movement by the sight of her feet. They were long, slim, shapely and a beautiful golden brown. The nails were perfectly shaped and painted a pale pink which exactly matched the rosebuds on the bedspread. Beautiful feet. But not hers!

She tried wriggling the toes. They responded dutifully.

She stretched out her hands. Also golden brown with perfectly manicured pink nails. And slimmer. Her wedding ring, which had begun to dig into her flesh in recent years, now sat easily on her finger. There was a pale mark where a second ring usually sat. She looked at the shelf by the bed and there, sure enough, was a diamond ring – a solitaire – a big one. She looked more closely at her wedding ring. Wider and heavier than the ring she had worn for the last eight years.

Quickly, she slid out of bed and went over to the mirror. It was her own reflection, but changed, idealised. She was slimmer and shapelier than she had ever been before and tanned evenly all over. She turned sideways. Breasts high and full, no trace of sagging. Small waist. Stomach almost concave. Legs long and shapely with beautiful slim ankles. No stretch marks. God, she hadn't looked this good when she was sixteen!

She turned away, trying to work out what was going on. She didn't believe in heaven and hell. Had supposed that when she died she would just go to sleep and not wake up. But this must be it − heaven − the afterlife.

It was nothing like what she had expected. She realised that she had, in fact, no clear idea of what heaven ought to be like. The Church was very definite about hell, but rather vague about heaven. She had the impression there ought to be clouds and angels in long white gowns, probably playing harps. She never even thought about what sort of buildings there might be. Perhaps something on the lines of ancient Greek temples?

Not this, anyway. This extravagant, luxurious bedroom seemed unchristian somehow.

Perhaps heaven was whatever you wanted it to be. Certainly she was rather taken with her delightful new body. This room was furnished very much to her taste, even if it was a bit over the top − sort of Laura Ashley for millionaires.

She could see the reflection of the bed in the mirror, and she noticed two things − there was a dressing gown on the bed, which she hadn't at first seen, as it was in the same white and rosebud silk as the bedspread. It was pretty well-camouflaged and she had only noticed it because of the way the light fell slanting through the window. The other thing she noticed was that there were two heaps of clothes, one on each side of the bed. With some trepidation, she went over and shrugged on the dressing gown, which fitted perfectly and felt wonderfully opulent against her bare skin. Then she bent down and checked the clothes.

On her side, a skimpy linen dress and some extravagant white lacy underwear. On the other side, a man's discarded shirt, socks and underpants. She picked up the shirt. White linen, crumpled and sweat-stained. Smelling, in fact, quite strongly of sweat… And very large. Everything in this place seemed to be oversized except her. She was beginning to feel like Jack in *Jack and the Beanstalk*. Any minute now the giant might walk in.

Facing her, on this side of the bed, were three doors. She dropped the shirt back on the floor, her mouth twisted in a moue of distaste, and walked over to the middle door. It led to a stairwell with a wrought-iron spiral staircase descending. With a shudder, she closed the door. She hated that kind of staircase. It gave her vertigo being able to see through the steps to the drop below.

The door to the left opened onto the biggest bathroom she had ever seen. The floor was marble, the fittings of mahogany and gold – not real gold, surely? There was a separate shower stall, a toilet and a bidet and two washbowls set in a pink marble counter which extended along a whole wall. Part of the counter was a dressing table area with a small drawer at either side and one of those mirrors you see in film stars' dressing rooms – huge, with lights all around it. And – the pièce de résistance – a sunken bath with Jacuzzi fittings. Good God almighty!

The wall beyond the bath was one long window looking out over the sea. The view was spectacular.

She came out of the room in a trance-like state. She must be dreaming this. She tried the last door, opened it and entered a room that was the nearest thing to paradise she could imagine. It was a walk-in wardrobe full of designer clothes! Racks of them, arranged by colour. Beside each rack was a peg with matching handbags suspended from it, underneath was a drawer unit and beneath that a shoe rack. She pulled open the nearest drawer. It was full of beautiful, exquisite, extravagant underwear in the same colour range as the clothes on the rack above it. It had always been a dream of hers – to always have matching underwear. She pulled out a handful. They were tiny, skimpy things. Not the sort of thing she would normally wear at all. Some of them were thongs. She'd always assumed they'd be uncomfortable. Well, now was her chance to find out.

Feeling very wicked, she gathered up a selection and went back into the bathroom to try out the Jacuzzi.

~*~

Half an hour later, bathed, creamed, perfumed and dressed like a film star, she made her way gingerly down the iron staircase, clinging to the bannister and trying not to look down. The stairs ended in a long corridor with windows on one side looking out onto a mountainside, and a series of doors opposite. She opened one. It was a bedroom, apparently unoccupied, with a window overlooking the sea.

Two or three doors along was another staircase, but this one was like the one in *Gone with the Wind*. She ran her fingers along the bannister as she swept down it, thinking she really should be wearing a crinoline. At the bottom was an enormous entrance foyer, tiled with mosaic pictures and, would you believe, a fountain in the centre. To the right big double doors opened onto a vast open plan living area with white leather sofas and low coffee tables. To the left was a baronial dining room and beyond that the kitchen.

Coffee! Her stomach crimped with the desire for caffeine.

The kitchen was, like everything else in this place, enormous, with marble counters and stainless steel fittings. In the centre was a butcher's block with a stainless steel canopy above it. The fridge was one of those American jobs, reaching nearly to the ceiling, with two doors and an ice-dispenser on the side. Christine prowled around the room looking for a coffee machine. When she found it she was somewhat overawed by its complexity. It was like the ones in cafes, full of knobs and handles, and she looked at it helplessly, not sure where to start.

There was a ring at the door and a voice cried, "Man-eaters!"

Christine stood and watched with something like horror as a key turned in the lock and the door opened.

Standing on the doorstep was a small, plump woman with dark hair and a friendly smile. She didn't look much like a man-eater.

"Oh, hello, Mrs Epstein," she said. "Not at the gym today?"

She spoke with a slight foreign accent, too slight for Christine to guess what it was.

"Er . . ." Christine put her hand to her forehead, unable to think of a single thing to say.

"You are not feeling well?" The woman came up to Christine staring into her eyes with an expression of concern. She was wearing a navy blue overall, like a shop assistant's. On the right breast was the logo MANITAS. On the left was a badge with 'Simona' in gold letters,

"I will make you coffee, yes?"

Christine found her voice. "Oh, yes, please."

She watched carefully as Simona pulled out a little cup shaped like a pan with a straight handle, filled it with ground coffee, pushed it back into place on the machine and pressed a button on the side. A red light came on and the machine began to make burbling noises. Simona put a mug under the dispenser and turned round with a smile. "You go and sit outside. I will bring it to you."

Christine nodded gratefully and went out of the door. She was on a broad terrace facing the sea, with a swimming pool on a slightly lower level. There was a pergola with bougainvillea climbing riotously overhead, a double swing seat and a wrought iron table with a tiled top. She sat down and looked out over the sea.

Mrs Epstein? Presumably Mr Epstein was the owner of the shirt and underwear on the floor upstairs. Simona was – what? – the cleaner? – the housekeeper?

From an agency. She remembered the overall with the logo. And she, Christine, was supposed to be at the gym. Did she work there? Or just work out? What did she *do* exactly?

Simona fetched the coffee. It was black. Christine smiled up at her. "Do you think I could have milk and sugar?" she asked.

Simona gave a surprised blink, but went back in the house and returned a moment later with a milk jug and a sugar bowl.

Christine added milk and sugar and took a blissful sip. Ah, that was more like it.

Ten minutes later she went back in the house to tackle the coffee machine herself.

While she waited for it to brew, she explored the breakfast possibilities. The fridge contained five pots of zero fat yoghurt, a cellophane pack of celery – opened, half a pint of skimmed milk, a plastic container of low fat spread and an apple. It was unbelievable! A fridge the size of a garage with virtually nothing in it! She looked in the freezer side. All the drawers were empty. Baffled, she searched the cupboards. Most of them contained crockery and glassware, but the cupboard above the coffee machine contained, besides coffee, a packet of teabags and an opened packet of the kind of crisp bread that looks and tastes like polystyrene. No eggs, no butter, no cheese, not even any bread. What did they live on? She was horribly afraid she knew the answer.

This was definitely not, under any circumstances, her idea of heaven. The bedroom and the bathroom and the designer clothes were fine, but she would never choose to live in a house with a spiral staircase. She would never have chosen a kitchen like this – all stainless steel and no food. And she would not, definitely not, live a life that involved going to the gym.

There had been a mix-up. She'd got stuck in the wrong life.

She went back outside, sat down at the table and leaned forward with her head in her hands. What the hell was she going to do?

~* ~

"Mrs Epstein?" It was Simona.

Christine looked up at her, aware that she must be acting very oddly.

"Are you feeling well? Is there anything I can do?"

Christine shook her head. "It's just," she said, "I'm hungry and there's no food in the house."

Simona looked surprised. Obviously there was never any food in the house.

"Would you like me to go to the shop," she asked, her small round face puckered with concern.

"Oh, would you," Christine said, feeling absurdly grateful.

"Sure." Simona smiled at her and Christine thought maybe this wasn't too bad after all. At least she wasn't looking at her as if she thought she was insane.

"What will I get?"

"Eggs," Christine said, "and bread and butter and..." she stopped for a moment while she thought about what she wanted. She was ravenous. "And bacon, and maybe some tomatoes."

Simona remained standing in front of her, smiling pleasantly, but obviously expecting something. Christine was at a loss for a moment and then realised – she needed money, of course. Oh, God. This place shouted of money but she hadn't the faintest idea where to find any. In her old life – her real life – she just had one handbag with her purse in it. She thought of all the handbags in the wardrobe upstairs, arranged by colour with the matching clothes and shoes. It seemed unlikely that she kept money in each one.

She looked helplessly at Simona.

"Will I get your purse?" Simona said.

Oh, what a treasure she was!

"Yes, please," Christine said and watched carefully as Simona went back into the house through the big front door and turned to the left. She was back in moments, carrying a small black leather wallet, which she passed to Christine.

Christine opened it. It was a card wallet with a money folder and a zipped compartment for coins. In the money folder was a thick wad of bank notes. She pulled them out and handed them to Simona.

"I only need one of these, Mrs Epstein," Simona said, laughing. And she peeled a note from the wad and passed the rest back.

"Take two," Christine said, "Just in case." She almost added, "and please call me Christine," but stopped herself just in time. She had no idea whether the Mrs Epstein whose body she was inhabiting would be so familiar with the staff, or even, indeed, if she was called Christine.

Simona shook her head, but accepted another note, then walked off round the side of the house.

A moment later Christine heard a car starting up and pulling away.

She went back into the kitchen and poured another cup of coffee. It looked OK She seemed to have got the proportions right. Then she went back outside and tried to take stock.

She seemed to have been thrust into a different version of herself, some sort of doppelganger, but she had no access to this person's memories. What a complete cock-up! You'd think if this sort of thing were allowed to happen, you'd at least be given a few clues.

Right. She needed a plan of action. Clearly if she didn't get a grip on what was going on, she would end up in some sort of mental home. It might help if she had any idea of where she was. Certainly not in England. No English sea was ever that colour. The seas around England were generally a sort of brownish-grey. Her guess would be a Mediterranean country. She looked down at the bank notes in the wallet. They each said 20 euros. Definitely Europe then – Spain maybe, or Greece or Italy.

She thought about the logo on Simona's overall – MANITAS. What language was that? She had a feeling she ought to know what it meant. Or was it just someone's name? There was a Greek name Manolo wasn't there?

She was living in a rich man's mansion in an unknown country with no memory of how she got here and no idea even of her own name.

Well, she should be able to find something out, surely. There must be letters, diaries, and photographs. Surely she would be able to find out enough to keep up a reasonable pretence whilst she worked out a plan of action. Because she was certain of one thing. She had no intention of staying here.

By the time she had finished her coffee, Simona had returned and Christine went back in the house and started cooking an enormous breakfast.

~* ~

It was amazing, she thought, as she wolfed down the bacon and eggs. She couldn't understand why she was so hungry. At first she had thought it was the usual raging hunger she got with a hangover. After all, she had drunk three bottles of wine last night. And then she thought, but not in this body. This body was, apparently, used to eating very little. But then, maybe you still felt hungry. Maybe the poor woman was hungry all the time. Christine shuddered at the thought and carried on eating. These really were the nicest eggs she had ever tasted.

She cleared her plate then loaded the dirty dishes in the dishwasher. She felt so much better now she had eaten something and had a plan. The first thing was to search the house for clues.

She did the ground floor first. The dining room had pictures on the walls, but they were all paintings and prints – no photographs. Same in the big living room. But they didn't live in there, surely. There must be a little, cosy room somewhere with a television and a music system. Beyond the living room was a corridor with a glass wall to the left revealing an indoor pool. To the right were two doors. Behind the first was an aggressively masculine study. All green leather and dark oak, with bookshelves lining the walls and a huge open fireplace with a stone hearth. What pictures there were were watercolours of English landscapes - very gentlemen's club.

The other room was smaller, cosier and decidedly more feminine. Definitely her own study. Comfortable stuffed furniture and a pine desk with a laptop and a printer on it. Christine had never been able to afford a laptop and, indeed, had very little experience of computers at all, having spent most of her adult life so far as wife, mother and factory worker. At the thought of her children a dreadful pang gripped her, and she wanted to hold them with a physical need that was almost painful. She gripped her stomach and bent over with the force of it. "Oh, God, what have I done?" she thought. "I can't live without them. And what will they do without me? Whatever made me think it was all right to leave them? I must have been insane."

And that was true, of course. She had been insane. And now she was paying the price. "I got here," she thought. "I can get back." And standing there racked with guilt was not going to help her. She had to get grip of this other Christine's life before the big man who owned the sweaty shirt came home.

Gritting her teeth, she pulled open the drawers of the desk one after another. Printing paper, pens, writing pads. But no letters, no diary, no photographs, no bills with her name on. "Oh, shit," she muttered, looking helplessly at the computer, which surely contained all the information she needed, but which she didn't even know how to switch on.

Somewhere in the depths of the house, a vacuum cleaner was switched off. She hadn't even noticed the sound of it until it stopped. She looked round the room. No photographs. No – wait. There was a photograph. Just one, on the mantelpiece. A wedding photo. Herself in a wonderful Cinderella gown, and a very large man in a morning suit. A very large man. Very tall, very wide, with a round moon face and big lips. He was smiling at the camera, and his lips split his face almost in two. She was irresistibly reminded of Mr Toad.

Oh, God. She was married to this horribly ugly man. Suddenly everything fell into place. She was a trophy wife! This explained the low fat yoghurt and the celery, the visits to the gym. She had to be beautiful and stay beautiful or she would be replaced by a younger model. She was overwhelmed by pity for her poor alternative self. Surrounded by luxury and unable to enjoy it. Living a dreadful empty life with no love in it. No amount of money could possibly compensate for that. This Christine, if indeed she was called Christine, had no children and apparently no pets. There was no sign of a cat or dog in the house. Not even any bloody fish. Not that she liked fish.

She stood in the middle of the room feeling lost and lonely. She had absolutely no idea what to do next.

His study, she thought. There must at least be bills somewhere, surely. She didn't like the idea of going through his things, but she had no choice.

She turned to leave the room just as Simona walked in.

"I'm off now, Mrs Epstein," she said. "Is there anything you want before I go?"

Christine shook her head. She could hardly say, "Yes, could you tell me my name, please. And that of my husband?"

"No, that's fine, Simona," she said. And just stopped herself from asking when she would be back. Her doppelganger would already know, of course.

Simona turned to go.

"Oh, there is one thing." Simona turned back, her eyebrows raised in a question.

"What does Manitas mean?" Christine pointed at the logo on Simona's overall.

The girl looked down at the logo and then looked up again with a smile. "It is Spanish for 'little hands'," she said. "It's the name of the agency."

"Of course," Christine said. "I knew I ought to know."

Simona gave her one last shy smile and then walked out of the room.

"Spain, then," Christine thought. "I'm in Spain." It wasn't much, but it was something.

Simona reappeared at the door. "Oh, I forgot to say. I met the postman on the way back from the shop. I've left the letters on the table by the door."

Oh, joy.

"Thank you, Simona," she said, and drew in a long breath.

As soon as she heard the car go down the drive, she went in search of the table by the door. The front door, surely? If it were the kitchen, she would have said so.

Sure enough, to the right of the front door was a small telephone table with a drawer. It must be the same place Simona had gone to earlier to get her purse. Next to the phone were a couple of letters.

"Oh, thank you, God," she said out loud, and reached for them.

The first one was addressed to Don Richard Epstein. The second, with an English stamp on it, was to Mr R Epstein, esquire.

She was confused. Which was it, Don or Richard? Perhaps his first name was Don, but he went by his second name?

"No, no, stupid," she said. "Don is a Spanish title, isn't it? Like Don Juan and Don Quixote. His name is Richard."

But she realised, with a drop of her heart that it still wasn't enough. What did she call him? Richard? Richie? It could even be Dick or Dickie. Or even, Heaven forbid, some pet name she couldn't even guess at - Binky or something equally nauseating.

And what about her? There was nothing to give her a clue about her own name. Mr Toad could come home any minute and she had no idea what to say to him. And what about – a feeling of dread crept over her – what happened AFTER he got home. What would he expect? She could feel panic taking over and forced herself to take long, slow breaths.

Just at that moment the phone began to ring. She looked at it with a kind of horror, as if it were a poisonous snake. The sound echoed around the stairwell, swelling until it seemed there was nothing in the world but the insistent shrill ringing.

Then it stopped. There was a click, and a man's voice said, "Ricky and Chrissie are not available at the moment, but you know what to do. One of us will get back to you as soon as we can."

It was a pleasant, deep, melodic voice. The Toad had probably paid some radio presenter or someone to record it for him. But she had the names. Thank you, God.

"Chrissie, are you there?" To her amazement, it was the same voice as the recording. "I've been trying to get you on your mobile. Have you let the battery go flat again?" He didn't sound angry, just amused. "Listen, I'm going to be late, Poppet. Can you make your own way there...What?" – he broke off, obviously talking to someone else in the room. "Look, I'll get back in a minute."

And he hung up.

Oh, God. Make her own way where? All the triumph she felt at finding out their names dissipated and she found herself shaking with fear. What was she going to do? He was expecting her to go somewhere and she hadn't a clue where.

The phone rang again, its shrill tone drilling through her head, and she backed away from it.

The answer phone cut in again and the Toad came back on the line. "It's OK, Chrissie. Ted's going to cover. Can you be ready at seven? I'll fetch you."

She sagged with relief and looked at her wrist. She wasn't wearing a watch! Bugger! She tried to remember whether she had seen a clock anywhere in the house. The living room. Surely there must be one in there. Sure enough, there was a rather ornate specimen on the mantelpiece, flanked by matching candlesticks.

She looked at the time in disbelief. Five o' clock! It couldn't be. What had happened to the day? Of course she had no idea what time it had been when she woke up.

Feeling very shaky and panicky, she went over to the clock and put her ear to it. It was ticking, so chances were it wasn't just for ornament.

She had two hours to get ready. She gritted her teeth and steeled herself to face the spiral staircase again.

Under normal circumstances two hours would be more than adequate, but she felt she would need every minute for this.

~* ~

At ten minutes to seven, bathed, creamed, perfumed, deodorised, her hair shampooed, conditioned and blow-dried, and her face made-up as perfectly as she knew how, she stood in front of the cheval mirror and took stock of herself. She was beautiful. So beautiful she took her own breath away. It was amazing what diet, exercise and expensive make-up could achieve. Now for the clothes!

She chose a stunning red dress in raw silk with a fine wavy white stripe, wicked matching lace underwear, matching red sling-back shoes and glove-leather handbag.

There was something missing. Of course – jewellery. A woman in her position probably wouldn't be seen dead without jewellery. There was the engagement ring, of course, on the bedside table, and she slipped it on while she looked round for a jewel box. There wasn't one. Perhaps it was kept in a safe somewhere. But in the drawer beneath the bedside table was a very nice gold watch and she decided that would have to do.

One last look in the mirror and she would go downstairs and wait for the Toad.

She heard the door downstairs open and a voice – the voice – called up the stairs. "Chrissie, are you up there?"

She froze, unable to move or speak, staring helplessly at her reflection, as she listened to the Toad coming up the stairs. The door opened behind her and she saw his reflection in the mirror. "Oh God, Chrissie," he said. "I was really worried you weren't going to be here. Are you OK?"

He put his arms around her. Instantly she felt herself enfolded in warmth. "SAFE," she thought. As if the word had been a password, memories came flooding into her head. She was Chrissie and he was Ricky. They DID have pet names – Poppet and Boo. They had been married for five years and had lived in Spain for the last two. Tonight they were going to a party at the Wilsons. It was very important to Ricky. He was in real estate and there would be lots of business associates there. It was her job to butter them up. She had been doing it for years and she was very good at it.

Lots of tiny details came tumbling through her mind, threatening to overwhelm her with too much input, but the amazing – the overpowering thing – was that she was not a trophy wife. She loved this man. She turned in his arms and kissed him, relishing his man smell and the feel of him against her. "Sorry, Sweetheart," she said into his chest. "I just didn't seem to get my act together today."

~*~

Later she thought about what had happened and wondered if it was like putting your SIM card in a different phone. The SIM card had all the information on it, but the phone might have its own memory and as soon as you put in your pin, you could access it. Somehow, when Ricky had taken her in his arms, the pin had been entered and she had picked up all the memories stored in this other body. But right now she was so relieved to be in control again that she didn't question how she knew.

All the way in the car she concentrated on the people she was going to meet at the party and what she needed to say. She had a job to do and couldn't allow herself to be distracted. But Ricky's presence beside her was disturbing. She was intensely aware of him, and could barely suppress a desire to touch him. She dared not look at him because she knew, knew without looking, that he felt the same thing, and it was so powerful she thought he might just drive the car off the road.

At last they arrived and Christine got out of the car and looked up at the Wilsons' imposing mansion. It was even bigger than theirs and this evening it was festooned in coloured flashing lights.

"Very tasteful," she murmured, and Ricky snorted with laughter behind her.

"Come on, you," he said, taking her arm. "Once more into the breach and all that."

A thrill passed through her as he touched her and she had to exercise every ounce of control she possessed not to grab him and head for the nearest bushes. Who would have thought she could have been so attracted to another man? Only yesterday she had killed herself because Kevin didn't love her anymore and now when she thought of him she felt nothing at all. No love, no hate, no anger – nothing at all. It was rather sad. She shook the thought away, but it had had the effect of distracting her and she was able to go into the house in a more equable frame of mind.

~*~

The ballroom – it had to be called that – it was too grand to be anything else – was thronged with people and she and Ricky had to force their way through to the far end where there was a bar complete with barman and a long buffet table with a vast array of food, attended by waiters and waitresses. She realised she was starving again and gratefully accepted a plate of dainties proffered by a passing waiter. Richard raised an eyebrow as she put a savoury biscuit in her mouth and managed to eat it with a degree of elegance. "I'm starving," she whispered, popping another biscuit into his mouth as she spoke. He swallowed the biscuit and then bent to kiss the top of her head. "Eat as much as you can, Poppet," he whispered back.

Another memory came in sharp and clear. She was anorexic, hence the lack of food in the house. She was afraid of food. Had been for years. And Richard had been quietly encouraging her to eat normally. But she would deal with all that later. Right now she needed to keep her wits about her.

~* ~

Richard pointed out a couple standing near the bar. He was very tanned and wearing an open-necked shirt, she had improbably black hair cut in a pageboy close to her head and so shiny that it looked as if it had been painted on. "That's them," he murmured. "Right," she thought. "The Hendersons." They were visiting the Wilsons and looking at possibly buying a place of their own. This could be a very big commission for Ricky.

Smiling at him, she made her way over to them. She heard Ricky give a small gasp as she turned away and she knew that he was as charged as she was. The knowledge gave her an entirely satisfying sense of her own power. The Hendersons had no chance of resisting her. Tonight she was invincible.

~* ~

All the way home in the car she avoided looking at Ricky, hugging her triumph with the Hendersons to herself. She had engaged them in conversation and they had told her how impressed they were with Marbella and how much they would like a house there, but there seemed to be very little on the market in their price bracket. She had commiserated with them and asked them what they were looking for exactly. Yes, there were very few houses of that size and grandeur on the open market, but maybe her husband could help. He was in real estate and had a lot of inside knowledge. She arranged for him to call on them tomorrow, and then set about learning all about their family. Nothing pleased people more than talking about themselves. She had memorised everything they said and now had it written down in her little notebook for Ricky to read later.

She was aware once again of the tremendous magnetism between them and shifted slightly in her seat, not looking at him, not touching, just waiting till they got home.

They almost made it to the front door. Richard abandoned the car at a crazy angle in the drive, leapt out of the car with surprising ability for such a big man and pulled her up and out of the passenger seat and into his arms. "Oh, Chrissie, I could hardly keep my hands off you all night," he groaned, running his lips along the base of her neck and crushing her to him. "Oh, Chrissie, Darling."

They got as far as the swing seat on the terrace.

~* ~

Christine awoke to bright sunshine and a shower of red petals falling around her like confetti. For a moment she couldn't imagine where on earth she was, and then she found the man next to her, the big man with the beautiful voice who had seduced her and almost made her forget her other family. The thought of the children still filled her with pain and longing, but as far as Kevin was concerned she was completely numb. She couldn't even remember what it felt like to love him – wasn't sure that she ever had loved him really. Not now that she had experienced the real thing. She looked at Ricky with genuine affection, his face was crumpled in sleep and his hair was tousled. He looked like a child himself. Admittedly, a very large child.

She turned around and gently pressed herself against his back, snuggling into the bulk of him, gently so as not to wake him, and gave herself over to sorting through her new memories. Her memories and Chrissie's seemed to be the same up to the age of sixteen or so.

The first obvious difference was that Chrissie had refused to stay on at school and do her A levels. She had fought her parents tooth and nail to let her go to fashion school and learn to be a model. She had put together a portfolio and had launched herself on the fashion scene before Christine had even started her history degree. Her father had ranted and railed, said it was a waste of good brains. Her mother had openly wept and said she didn't want her daughter to go to one of those arty places where she would meet hippies and end up addicted to drugs and pregnant.

Christine smiled. She herself had got pregnant half way through her second year at Manchester, abandoned her degree and married a feckless poet, whereas Chrissie had made it. She had remodelled herself, dieted and exercised the old Christine out of existence and hit the catwalks with a fanfare that still echoed in the fashion world. She was at the top of her profession when she met Ricky, jet-setting from one assignment to another, and her parents' anxieties were by then assuaged. "She can always go to university and get proper qualifications later," her father had said, bemused by the vast amounts of money she was earning. Her mother was worried about how thin she was getting, but delighted by the fact that she was mingling with the rich and famous, hopeful for a suitable marriage. Sweet old things. They still seemed to inhabit some pre-sixties world with pre-war values.

Meeting Ricky had changed everything. She lost interest in fashion. She couldn't bear to be away from him so often. He accompanied her when he could, but his own very successful and lucrative business in the high end of estate agency needed a lot of attention. When they married, she gave up her career without a second thought or a single regret.

The only problem was that she had been slowly sinking into anorexia all the time she had been modelling. It was an occupational hazard. Everyone in the industry was obsessed with weight and dieting – and not just the models. The designers were just as bad, and the fashion journalists. People she knew had literally died of starvation. But knowing how dangerous it was and dealing with it were two different things. She had thought nothing of it, put it down to the stress of all the travelling and hard work. Lots of her friends had the same symptoms. Now she knew it was because they were all starving themselves.

After she married Ricky, she was horrified to discover that she was unlikely to be able to conceive children because she had damaged her reproductive organs. "They're the first thing to go," her doctor had said, shaking his head sympathetically. "When did you notice that you had stopped menstruating?"

Ricky had been wonderful, understanding and considerate. He said it didn't matter about the children, they could always adopt. What mattered was learning to like food again. She tried to explain that she didn't dislike food, she thought about it all the time, longed for it, but was afraid to eat it. He said they would take it one step at a time. He tempted her with different things, just small amounts, nothing that would make her fat. And she did get a little better, but not much. So they moved to Spain, away from London and her smart fashion industry friends who thought it was normal to look like a famine victim. And Ricky had set up a new business here, pandering to wealthy people who wanted to show off their wealth.

They didn't need the money. Between them they had already made enough to keep them in luxury for the rest of their lives, but Richard enjoyed his work and his clients were dazzled by his celebrity wife.

It was interesting that she seemed to have completely lost her fear of food now the other Christine had taken over. It seemed to have nothing to do with the physical and everything to do with the emotional. Christine had picked up Chrissie's memories, but none of her hang-ups. She realised, in fact, that she was hungry right now.

"Ricky," she said, leaning over and blowing in his ear. "Boo, do you fancy some breakfast? I'm going to make bacon and eggs."

Ricky's eyes flew open and he sat up, nearly overturning the swing seat and throwing them both to the ground.

"What did you say?" A slow grin spread over his face as she repeated the offer. "Would I! Yes please. Please." And he hugged her so fiercely she feared for her ribs.

~* ~

The next few days passed in a whirl of delight. It was like a second honeymoon. Indeed, for Christine it was a first honeymoon. It had never been like this with Kevin. She hadn't known it could be like this. Full-on Mills and Boon stuff. She became obsessed with sex. When Ricky was at the office she had to restrain herself from ringing him up every few minutes. She spent the day working out and preparing herself for him, behaving in fact exactly like Chrissie, except in her case it was to fill in time until he came home.

And she ate. She went food shopping every day, revelling in the wonderful fresh fruit and vegetables, so much more flavoursome than the tired excuses for vegetables she was used to in England. She indulged herself with gourmet food, gorging herself on foie gras, fillet steak and lobster. And she filled out a bit.

She wasn't getting fat, just curvaceous. Ricky loved it.

"You don't think I'm getting too fat?" she asked, standing in front of the mirror and turning round to look at herself.

"Fat!" he exclaimed. "You're gorgeous. You get more beautiful every day."

"That's all very well," she said, pouting slightly, "but if it goes on like this, none of my clothes will fit me."

Ricky shrugged. "So buy some more. Now come here."

The obsession with sex became so all-consuming that they decided to take a holiday as soon as the Henderson project was completed. He had found a suitable property for them and they were delighted with it. A great monstrosity of a place with turrets like a fort, perched on top of a hill overlooking the bay. At night it was under-lit with sodium lights, giving it a Disney World aspect. Heaven knows what the poor neighbours suffered. The purchase of the house was well underway, deposit paid, solicitor engaged, and the rest could easily have been left to another member of staff, but clients of the Henderson's stature required the personal attention of the managing director and Ricky had to see it through himself.

Christine sat it out with barely-concealed impatience and revelled in their nights together.

She realised with a guilty pang that she hardly ever thought about her children these days. It still hurt to remember them, but it wasn't the overwhelming

pain it had been at first, and she comforted herself
with the knowledge that her mother would look after
them, probably better than she had herself. She had,
after all, devoted most of her time to Kevin.

~* ~

Three months later they finally got away. "Where
are we going?" she had asked him, but he shook his
head and touched his nose in an 'I know, but I'm not
telling' gesture. They went in a Lear Jet – not
Richard's, he wasn't interested in flying and didn't
need a private plane for the business, most of which
was concentrated in Spain. It belonged to a friend
who did fly and was only too happy to transport them
to a secret destination – well, secret to Christine,
anyway.

She knew nothing of geography and so looking
out of the window gave her no clues. Within a very
short time she had even lost track of their general
direction. But she didn't care. It was wonderful being
with Ricky on holiday - no clients to worry about –
nothing to think about except each other. She tipped
her glass of champagne towards him. "Salute!" she
said and he laughed at her. "It's 'salud'," he said,
"health." And he touched her glass with his. She felt a
mild thrill at even this slight contact. Who would
have thought it could remain so intense?

He seemed so handsome to her now. A big,
handsome, sexy man. She could hardly believe that
the first thing she had thought of when she had seen
his photograph was Mr Toad. It must have been a
hangover from the pathetic Kevin, who had been,

39

let's face it, skinny and flabby. He was, in fact, the ideal companion for the wimp Daphne. She hoped they were happy together, but doubted it. He was probably already embarking on his next muse. She smiled a wry smile.

"What are you thinking?"

She looked up into Ricky's lovely, beloved face and the smile broadened. "I was thinking how lucky I am," she said.

"And I," he said, "can't believe my luck. I wake up every day and marvel that I have you beside me. I love you so much."

He bent over to kiss her and spilled his champagne all over the pair of them. "Oh, shit," he said absently, wiping down first his own shirt and then hers. She put down her glass and kissed him back.

~* ~

They were on an island somewhere in the tropics – white sand, coconut palms, turquoise sea. The sun rose and set at exactly seven am and seven pm every day. They were in a bamboo hut with a wooden bed and very little else. Above them a huge wooden fan moved the air about, but didn't do much to lower the temperature. Every so often they went to bathe in the sea to cool off. When they were hungry they walked along the beach to a little cafe that sold snacks and cold drinks and where they could call for a taxi to take them somewhere more sophisticated.

They got very brown.

"I could do this forever," Chrissie said, lying on the wooden bed, looking up at the skylight overhead where three little geckos were walking about. They had tiny feet with perfect little toes spread out. Every so often one of them would suddenly take off at lightning speed to catch an insect.

"No, you couldn't," Ricky said, pushing a tendril of hair away from her face and brushing her cheek. "You'd get bored."

"Bored with you!" she said, shocked.

"Of course not. Although hardly a day goes by when I don't wonder why you don't. No, I mean bored with the inactivity."

"I wouldn't say we were exactly inactive," she said, looking at him through half-closed lids.

He grinned. "Yeah, I know. But I think after a while you'd want to do something more constructive."

She bent down and began to concentrate on stroking his thigh. "I think what we're doing is quite constructive enough for me."

"So you're not desperate to get back to the housing market in Marbella? What about all those lovely people like the Hendersons and the Wilsons?"

"Oh, shut up!" she said and gave him a playful smack.

She supposed they would have to go back soon, though. This didn't really feel like real life, just a hiatus.

~* ~

They spent their last night in the little beach cafe. The waiter served them with particular care, giving them a variety of delicious spicy dishes and serving glass after glass of wine. Christine had reached a stage of pleasant wooziness when Ricky suddenly sat forward and spat out a spray of wine. "My God, what's this!"

Christine looked at her own glass. She had already drunk it all. But she remembered thinking it was nowhere near as nice as the others. The waiter came hurrying across. "It is a special wine I got in just for you," he said, beaming all over his face. "From your own country. It says British, see?"

And he waved a bottle at them. Christine narrowed her eyes to read the label. *Concorde British Red Sparkling Wine.*

Oh, God. She had a very bad feeling about this. Ricky was smiling at the man, exerting his usual charm. "How thoughtful of you," he said. "It is delicious. But I think we have perhaps had enough to drink now."

He paid the bill and took Christine by the arm, walking her back towards their hut and giggling slightly. "That is, without doubt, the very worst wine I have ever tasted," he said. Christine tried to appear amused, but her stomach was churning with fear. "This is silly," she thought to herself, "It could hardly have been the wine that did it."

She clutched Ricky's arm more tightly and determined not to think about it. Anyway, she had only had one glass.

Her lovemaking that night was frenetic. "Hey," Ricky said, "Calm down. We've got all the time in the world."

And she slowed down, but she was very much afraid there was no more time – no more time at all.

After Ricky was asleep, she lay for a long time afraid to close her eyes, terrified she might somehow slip into another world and lose him. She traced the lineaments of his face in the moonlight, committing them to memory.

~* ~

Christine woke up to a white room. Not her own lovely, fairy-tale princess-in-the-tower room but a much smaller affair with shiny tiled walls covered in monitors and switches. My God! She was in a hospital!

There were tubes coming out of machines attached to various parts of her. She stretched out her arm. It was painfully thin and white, with a needle sticking in it. She tried to sit up, but felt too weak to make the effort. A voice said, "She's come round. She's awake." She heard the sound of rubber soles tapping on tiles as someone walked out of the room and down a corridor. The owner of the voice put a hand under her neck and helped her to rise up a little in the bed. It was a young woman in a nurse's uniform, her blond hair tied back under a little cap.

"Are you thirsty?" she asked. And Christine realised she was thirsty, had a raging thirst and a sore throat. "It'll be a hangover from all that wine," she thought, and then was suddenly gripped with panic.

What was she doing here? Was it the anorexia? Had she gone over some boundary that made them admit her to hospital? "My husband," she croaked, her voice a thin, rusty thread.

"It's all right." The nurse smiled. "He'll be here soon. They're just contacting him now. He's been very concerned about you."

Christine gave a nod and lay back gratefully among the pillows. She could sleep now she knew Ricky was on his way.

When she opened her eyes again, there was a thin little man sitting at the side of the bed. He saw she was awake and smiled at her. "Christine," he said, "Darling. I've been so worried."

She had had no idea who he was until he spoke, and then she realised with something like amazement that it was Kevin. She didn't remember him being this thin and white and, well, insipid. She was so disappointed she could hardly speak.

"What do you want?" she whispered.

His face took on a sad expression. "Darling, I just want to know you're all right. Sweetheart, I need you to get better and come home."

She stared at him in disbelief. "What about Daphne?"

He shrugged. "Oh that didn't mean anything. It was just a phase."

She continued to stare and he smiled his little boy smile, the one that used to make her heart turn over. "I need you to come home, Christine. I can't manage without you."

When she didn't reply, he went on. "You know I'm useless at keeping the show on the road. I haven't managed to pay the rent for the last six weeks."

Using all the strength at her command, she raised herself up in the bed. She looked at this man whom she used to love. This man who had fathered her children. For eight years she had cleaned his house, laundered his clothes, cooked his meals and gone out to work to support him. And in return he had betrayed her with the pathetic Daphne, and maybe Daphne wasn't the first – *probably* she wasn't the first.

She had all the words ready. Daphne might not mean anything to you, but she bloody well meant something to me. She destroyed me. But it was too hard and her throat was too sore, so she just said, "Watch my lips, Kevin." And then, eyes blazing, she spat out, "FUCK OFF."

Kevin backed off in surprise, made a half-hearted attempt at another little boy smile, then turned and walked quickly out of the room.

Christine lay back against the pillows again with a sigh.

She had a lot to do. Closing her eyes, she went over in her mind everything she knew about Ricky. He was thirty-five years old. He was born in Leeds. His birthday was the twenty-seventh of July. His parents were still alive. They were called Betty and Simon Epstein and they lived in Manchester in the Cheetham Hill area. He had tried to persuade them to move out to Spain, but they had refused to leave their friends and the home they had lived in all their married lives.

She was pretty sure she could find the house again. She visualised the street in her mind. Certain. She was certain she could find it. She would see her children first. The familiar pain swept over her, but this time it was tempered with anticipation instead of hopelessness. Then she would look for Ricky.

He existed in that other world. He must exist in this one. She would find him. She had been given this one, heaven-sent chance to have it all – to keep her children and her soul mate. Please God he hadn't married someone else. She pressed her lips together and lifted her jaw. If he had, it would be a mistake. *She* was his soul mate and she would fight tooth and nail to get him.

And she would never, ever, drink Concorde British Red Sparkling Wine again.

THE END

ABOUT THE STORY

Six years ago I wrote *Doppelganger* as my submission to an anthology. The theme of the anthology was 'What if you had made a different decision? What would your life be like?

Well, I have been obsessed with alternative dimensions ever since I first read John Wyndham's short stories, and this theme simply cried out for an alternative dimension interpretation.

I live in a house a bit like Christine's Spanish house in the story. Not quite as luxurious, but our house overlooks the sea on one side and the mountains on the other.
I have not, however, as far as I know, ever gone into a different dimension.

The story was so well-received that it was subsequently published in a different anthology and then as a stand-alone book before achieving its present incarnation as an independently published story.

But several readers said they wanted more. They wanted to know what happened to Christine when she returned to her own dimension. The most persistent of these was my friend Tara Fox Hall, who must have asked me dozens, maybe hundreds of times.

So I wrote a sequel, Flipside.

Flipside

A sequel to Doppelganger

By Jenny Twist

Credits

Editor: Emily Eva Editing

Dedication

For my dear friend, Tara Fox

Hall

"It is never too late to be what you might have been."
Attributed to George Eliot

Flipside

Richard

The door slammed and Richard remained slumped over his desk with his head in his hands, Jacqueline's final accusatory words ringing in his ears. "I'm not good enough for your posh family and your wealthy friends!"

Pain pulsed behind his left eye. It had been happening more frequently lately and he had begun to wonder whether it might be the first symptoms of a brain tumour.

He groaned. Another relationship down the pan. What was the matter with him? Other people managed to make a go of it. It was his own fault, he knew. He had absolutely no experience of women. He'd been too busy making money.

~ * ~

Richard had left school at sixteen, to the chagrin of his parents, who had cherished hopes of university for their clever son. But he'd had enough of education. He knew what he wanted to do and he didn't need a degree to do it. So he had left and gone to work in an estate agent's. He started as general office boy but soon displayed such an aptitude for choosing and selling properties that he became a fully-fledged agent. He was good at it and made good commissions, but that wasn't where the real money was. With his parents' help he had got together the mortgage for a run-down property in an area which he just knew was about to become fashionable and had spent every free waking moment doing it up. When he sold it a year later, at a thundering great profit, he had used the money as a deposit on three more houses and done the same thing again, this time employing professional builders to do most of the work.

By the time he was twenty-five, Richard owned several streets of high-rent properties and had opened his own estate agency. By the time he was twenty-seven he had made his first million, his estate agency had a dozen branches and he also owned his own building firm. Now, at twenty-nine, he employed dozens of staff and had all his financial affairs handled by an accountant.

His parents had watched all this with a certain amount of bewilderment. He had paid back their original loan years before and tried without success to persuade them to let him buy them a nice detached house in the country.

"Certainly not," his mother had said. It had nothing to do with pride. His parents were happy and comfortable in their two-bedroomed terrace house in Cheetham Hill where they knew all their neighbours. "Maybe when we have grandchildren," she had said, with a meaningful look.

And therein lay the rub. In his obsession with making money he'd had no time for women. Apart from his mother, the only women he knew and liked were already married to friends of his. And he wanted someone who was available. It was only now that he could take a breather, so to speak, that he appreciated the hole in his life where a woman and maybe children should be. And it seemed he had left it too late. All the women he might have wanted were already married. He joined an on-line dating agency.

Jacqueline was the fifteenth woman he had contacted. She was pleasant enough, quite good-looking, reasonably intelligent, better than most of the others he had met, but the spark he thought ought to be there wasn't. They had become increasingly irritated with each other, mainly because he didn't want to commit. He just couldn't do it. She wasn't right and he knew she wasn't. But he couldn't say so without hurting her feelings. He began to feel trapped.

Their final, deadly row, the one that made her storm out of the office and slam the door behind her, had been over his failure to introduce her to his parents.

"You're ashamed of me, aren't you?" she demanded, her face ugly with anger. "I'm not good enough for your posh family and your wealthy friends!" And she ran out of the room, the back of her hand pressed against her mouth, tears beginning to run down her cheeks. Useless to try to explain that his friends and family were neither posh nor wealthy. It was nothing to do with that. She just wasn't *right* and he didn't want the embarrassment of introducing her to everyone and then later having to explain that it hadn't worked out.

That night for the first time he dreamt of a woman with dark blonde hair.

His mother was sympathetic but pragmatic.

"For goodness' sake, Richard. You're a young man. You've got all the time in the world. I don't mind waiting a few more years for grandchildren." She gave him a meaningful look. "You are being careful to make sure there are no *unwanted* grandchildren, aren't you?"

"*Mother!* I don't need to worry about that. All the girls are on the pill these days."

"I'm sure they are," she said dryly, "but it wouldn't be the first time a girl had been careless in order to trap a wealthy man."

He felt a small trickle of disquiet. How many times had he taken that risk? Could Jacqueline even now be incubating his child? He shook his head. Surely not. Jacqueline was a nice girl with principles. But he vowed never again to be so careless.

That night he dreamt of the woman with dark blonde hair again. He was leaning over her sleeping face, marvelling at the perfection of her skin, the line of her eyebrows, the curve of her lips.

Her eyes flew open. They were bright, electric blue. She smiled up at him. "Ricky," she said and reached up to stroke his face.

He dreamt of her the next night and the night after that. It didn't feel like a dream at all. In fact it began to feel more real than his waking life. Every night the dream took up from where it left off the night before. He had heard of recurring dreams, but never serial dreams. It was as if he stepped out of his familiar, mundane life and stepped into another life, just as real, whenever he went to sleep. He started going to bed earlier so as to spend more time with her.

In the dream he had a full set of memories. She was called Chrissie. She had been a fashion model when he met her, at the top of her game. Her face was on all the magazines and she was earning a fortune.

They met at a party thrown by one of Richard's high-flying clients. He had been standing at the bar, feeling out of place and drinking a dreadful cocktail which appeared to consist of creosote and orange juice. And he had looked up to see this vision of loveliness approaching him with a determined expression on her face. She gave him a brief smile as she leant across the bar to ask for a cocktail, then she turned round and stood next to him, taking a tentative sip.

"Ugh! What's in this? Jeyes fluid?"

Richard snorted with laughter and to his horror the mouthful of cocktail rose up his throat and exploded out of his mouth and even down his nose! Nothing like that had ever happened to him before.

"You sure have a way of making an impression on a girl," she said, as she passed him a paper napkin from the bar.

"Oh, don't," he said. "Don't make me laugh again."

She looked him over with a cool, appraising glance. "You don't seem to fit in with this crowd."

"One of my clients invited me. Not my scene at all." Recklessly he took another sip of the vile

cocktail and spluttered, but less dramatically than
before.

"Me too," she said. "Well, my agent. I'm so
bored I could spit."

Richard grinned at her.

She put her glass back on the bar with a
purposeful air. "What do you say we check out of this
dump and find a real bar and drink beer?"

"Aren't you supposed to mingle?"

She swept the room with a disdainful glare.
"If I have to mingle for one more minute I shall lose
the will to live."

"Oh, please don't."

They held hands and sneaked away. Although
it wasn't really possible to sneak with Chrissie.
Richard noticed every head swivel towards them as
they walked out, the men looking with desire, the
women with envy. He felt a tremendous pride having
such a beauty on his arm.

Later they went back to her Mayfair flat.
"Bloody hell," said Richard as he stepped through
the door onto a deep pile cream carpet.

"This isn't where I live," she said. "This is
just a pied-à-terre."

"Where do you live?"

She laughed. "With my mum and dad in
Alderley Edge."

"You're joking!" He realised now why his
own Manchester accent had seemed to get stronger as
the evening progressed. "I'm from Cheetham Hill."

"God, we used to live in Harpurhey."

"You're kidding!"

"No, really." She gave a small, ladylike hiccup. "I bought my parents the house in Alderley Edge when the money started rolling in." She paused. "But I'm not sure they like it as much. I think they miss the neighbours."

"My mum refused to move out of Cheetham Hill," said Richard. "She said she was happy there and had no intention of moving in with strangers."

"Well, there you are," said Chrissie.

Two months later they married.

The only fly in the ointment was that Chrissie was suffering from anorexia. It was an occupational hazard in her profession. "They all are," she said. "Not just the models. The designers, the fashion journalists – all of them."

He tried to help her. He encouraged her to eat a little bit at a time. Eventually he persuaded her to move to Spain, away from her famine victim friends.

She fretted that the anorexia had probably rendered her infertile but he was unperturbed. "So we adopt," he said. He really didn't mind. He loved children. They didn't have to be his own.

Just lately she'd been eating normally. His heart leapt when he saw her putting on a little extra weight. She had been beautiful before, with a kind of wraith-like, ethereal beauty. Now she had the shapely, mature beauty of a Marilyn Monroe. God, he loved her.

And then, one day, for no reason, it stopped.

~ * ~

He couldn't believe it. He woke up without visiting his other life. At first he thought it would come back but it didn't. Night after night he went to sleep and woke up without seeing her. He was beside himself with despair. No use telling himself she was just a figment of his imagination, something made up by his own subconscious to comfort him. She was as real to him as the people in his waking life. More real than most of them. He mourned her as if she were a living person who had died. He couldn't even ask for sympathy from his friends. He would just look like a lunatic.

He couldn't believe she was only a dream. Despite his dislike of social media, he searched for her on Google — millions of Christine Jones, no Chrystal J, her professional name. Same with Facebook.

Still reluctant to give in, he went to her parents' house in Alderley Edge. A young woman with a baby on her arm answered the door. When he asked about Mr and Mrs Jones, she looked at him blankly.

"Perhaps they were the previous owners?" he suggested.

The woman shook her head. "Can't have been. We were the first people to live here. Maybe you've got the wrong street."

He hadn't got the wrong street. In his sleep he had been here dozens of times. He had the wrong bloody life.

~ * ~

He stayed at home, only leaving his flat for unavoidable obligations. His regular weekend trips to his parents diminished. His mother worried about him.

"What is it? A love affair gone wrong?"

"You could say that," he replied and didn't elucidate any further.

One of his unavoidable obligations was his quarterly visit to his accountant. They spent an hour or so discussing his financial affairs, or rather Simon told him exactly what was happening and he listened. They generally had lunch together afterwards. They were friends as well as business associates. Simon had a delightful, intelligent young wife and two perfect children, one of whom was Richard's godson. Another friend who was happily married.

He entered Simon's building, walked into the reception area and stopped dead, his heart hammering in his chest. Sitting at the reception desk was a girl with dark blonde hair. She was on the phone and had her face turned away from him but he was certain it was her. Then she put the phone down, turned and gave him a brief, professional smile. It wasn't her. This girl was pretty but she didn't have Chrissie's bone-deep beauty and if that were not enough to shatter the illusion, when she spoke it was with a broad, flat accent. "Can I help you?"

"I have an appointment with Mr Goldsmith," he said stiffly, annoyed with her for not being Chrissie.

"Name?"

"Richard Epstein, I expect it's written down in Mr Goldsmith's diary."

The girl's lower lip trembled and he felt ashamed of himself. It wasn't her fault she wasn't Chrissie.

"Mr Goldsmith told me to check," she said, turning away from him to look at her computer screen. When she turned back she had recovered herself. "Yes, here it is. You can go straight in."

He paused before turning away. "Sorry," he said. "I'm having a hard day. No need to take it out on you."

She gave him a brilliant smile, making him feel even more ashamed. "That's all right, Sir." And she turned back to her computer.

"Who's the girl?"

Simon frowned. "What girl?"

"The one on reception. The one with the dark blonde hair."

"Oh, Tracy? She's from the agency. Becky's on holiday. She's gone off to Ibiza with her boyfriend."

"Boyfriend! She must be a hundred years old!"

"She's fifty-two. That's nothing these days. Turns out she's been courting Alan Hacker, you know, the caretaker."

He didn't but he nodded.

"Well, he proposed marriage and she proposed a three week holiday on the grounds that if they could spend three weeks in each other's company twenty-four seven and could still stand the sight of each other when they got back, it would probably work out."

Richard exploded into laughter. "Good for her."

Simon pulled up a load of figures on his computer and began to deliver his quarterly lecture. Richard went into his customary trance. He enjoyed watching the money grow but the analysis bored him. His thoughts kept drifting back to the temporary receptionist. She wasn't Chrissie but she did have the advantage of being a real flesh and blood woman.

Tracy went straight to her screen and accessed Mr Goldsmith's diary. The entry for Richard Epstein had five stars next to it. *Whew! Mega important client!*

She gave a quick look round to make sure reception was still empty, then googled him. She thought there might be a lot of Richard Epsteins but Google was dominated by just two, an American lawyer and an English multi-millionaire property developer. There was a photograph of him and an entry in Wikipedia. Stunned, she sat back in her chair and read the whole entry from beginning to end. "Bloody hell!" she said aloud.

"I'm sorry. Have I come at a bad time?" Tracy gave a guilty start and instinctively closed the screen hoping he hadn't seen what was on it.

"Oh, hello, Mr Epstein. Sorry. I didn't hear you come in."

"Tracy, isn't it?"

She nodded, giving him her brightest smile.

"Look, I'd like to apologise for being so abrupt earlier. Can I make amends by taking you out to lunch?"

She was so flabbergasted she said the first thing that came into her head. "I only have an hour."

He smiled. "I didn't mean today. Maybe Saturday?" He passed her his card. "Give me a ring or email me and we'll fix a date. That is, if you want to."

She stared at him, the smile fixed on her face. "Yes, thank you. I'd like that. I'll call then, shall I?"

He looked at his watch. "Sorry. Have to go. I'm keeping Mr Goldsmith waiting." He smiled once more, then hurried out. Wondering, Tracy turned back to Wikipedia. *A multi-millionaire! Bloody hell!* Her thoughts turned to what she should wear to have lunch with a millionaire. No doubt he'd take her somewhere really posh.

Richard picked her up outside her house at midday on Saturday. She came to the door wearing a vivid scarlet dress in some shiny material. It was embarrassingly short and displayed a considerable amount of cleavage. He gasped. She gave him a smug smile. He smiled back.

"Sorry, but could I just use your facilities?"

"Of course." She directed him upstairs.

Bloody hell! He couldn't take her to Gino's dressed like that. There would be people there who knew him. He punched out Gino's number and turned on the tap to mask the sound.

"Gino? Listen, I'm going to have to cancel. I'm so sorry. Something's come up. I'll pay for the table of course."

"No need, Mr Epstein," Gino said cheerfully. "We're never very busy on a Saturday lunchtime. Nothing too distressing, I hope?"

"What? No, no. It's no big deal. Just something I can't get out of. Call you later." And he put the phone back in his pocket.

Shit! Where on earth was he going to take her? She looked like a bloody prostitute.

Tracy was very excited. She was looking her best. She'd bought a fabulous dress and matching red shoes with six inch heels. It had cost nearly a month's wages but it was worth it. You have to speculate to accumulate.

But it turned out it was all for nothing!

It started well. He picked her up in a BMW. But instead of taking her to some swanky restaurant, he took her to a country pub where she felt overdressed and stupid. She couldn't believe a millionaire would eat in a pub like a normal person. Perhaps he'd chosen it to make her feel at ease? If he hadn't been a millionaire she would have sulked but she put a brave face on it and smiled till her face felt as if it would crack.

Mr Epstein didn't speak much but he spent a lot of time just looking at her. She had the weirdest feeling that he was expecting something from her but she had no idea what it was.

Richard, on the other hand, could think of nothing to say. This girl looked good but she seemed to have no conversation at all and after a few attempts at small talk he found himself staring at her trying to see Chrissie in that face that was so similar but not quite the same.

Bearing in mind how offended Jacqueline had been, he had decided that he would ask Tracy to come and meet his parents at the first opportunity, but he couldn't quite bring himself to ask. He had a gut feeling that this was all a horrible mistake.

Three weeks later he plucked up the courage and asked her. "But could you, perhaps, wear something a little quieter? My parents are very old-fashioned."

She was offended but maintained her bright smile. "Of course," she said and after a couple of days of indecision decided to go for her office outfit. She had no choice anyway. She couldn't possibly afford to buy another outfit without borrowing money.

~ * ~

His parents were nice to her but not exactly effusive. After the initial greeting his father had lapsed into silence. His mother had been friendly and chatty but he could tell she didn't think much of his new conquest.

At the first opportunity his mother got him alone in the kitchen and whispered, "You be careful with that one. She's a gold-digger."

He stared at her, surprised and hurt. "Mother, do you think that I'm so ugly that no-one could fancy me if I didn't have a lot of money?"

His mother smiled and touched his cheek. "You know very well that I don't think that," she said. "You are handsome and intelligent and loving, and any girl in her right mind would jump at the chance to be your girlfriend. But that one" – her eyes cut to the living room door –"That one is jumping all right. But not at you. She's jumping at the money. Just be careful." And she patted him on the cheek.

He would have been annoyed except deep down he knew she was right. There had been small incidents. Casual suggestions that he should take her on an exotic holiday; that they should think about moving in together. In fact, she seemed to be surreptitiously doing just that. A couple of times when she stayed overnight in his flat he had found things she'd left behind – a make-up bag, a toothbrush, spare underwear.

He had handed them back to her next time he saw her and she was annoyed. "What does it matter? I stay there regularly. It won't do any harm to have a few things in case."

In case of what? he wondered. Did she think he would invite her to stay on for a few more days? He kept thinking about what his mother had said about girls who were careless and he began to be paranoid about the possibility of getting her pregnant. She was already upset that he used contraceptives. "You don't need that," she had said. "I'm on the pill."

"I believe a man should be responsible for his own contraception," he had said, knowing he sounded sententious. She had sniffed loudly and was less than enthusiastic in the love-making that followed. In a way that was a relief.

He took to hiding the contraceptives, afraid she might pierce them with a pin. Every so often he examined them surreptitiously for signs of interference.

He knew just how ridiculous he was being. He needed to end the relationship now before it got even worse. The pain pulsed behind his eye again.

~ * ~

The weekend was coming up and he had promised to take her out on Friday night. He was running out of places to go, terrified he might bump into someone he knew. Tonight he would finish it. Definitely, *definitely*. But he couldn't bring himself to say it and she ended up back at his flat again.

When he got out his contraceptives she frowned. "I hate those things. It's like eating a sweet with the wrapper on. I really don't know why you bother. I've told you I'm on the pill." She paused. "Or do you think I've got the clap?"

Oh, thanks very much, he thought. *Just what I need. Something else to worry about.*

It turned out not to be a problem after all. He lost all interest in love-making and resisted her attempts to arouse him. "No, please don't," he said, hot with embarrassment. "It's just that I'm really tired.

He lay awake for hours, embarrassed and angry with himself. Tracy snored softly beside him and he wished with all his heart that she'd just go away. He wanted Chrissie. No substitute would do. Definitely, in the morning, he'd tell her. *Definitely.*

~ * ~

The next morning the other half of the bed was empty and he entertained the cowardly hope that she had just gone away of her own accord. But no, the bedroom door opened and Tracy came in bearing a tray.

"Breakfast!" she called out brightly. She was wearing an almost see-through negligee and was fully made-up. It made him feel slightly sick.

She put the tray down on the bedside table and he leaned over to take a look.

"What the bloody hell's that?"

"Muesli with skimmed milk. I thought it'd be good to have a more healthy lifestyle."

"You can if you like," he muttered, reaching for the coffee.

He took a gulp and very nearly sprayed it out again. "What?" he began.

"It's decaffeinated. Where do you think you're going?"

Richard was half-way out of bed, shrugging into his dressing gown.

"I'm going to put the coffee machine on. Then I'm going to have a shower. Then I'm making a proper breakfast."

Later, as he got bacon and eggs out of the fridge, he realised she had still not emerged from the bedroom.

"You OK in there?" he called. "I'm making bacon and eggs. Do you want some?

She came out, still wearing the negligee, but her make-up was smudged with crying.

"No thanks," she said, putting the spurned tray down on the kitchen table and beginning to eat the muesli with quiet determination.

He felt a terrible guilt rising inside him and swiftly repressed it. Now was not the time to go wishy-washy. He really had to finish with her today.

He sat down in front of her with his plate of bacon and eggs with toast and coffee – real coffee from the espresso machine.

She looked up shyly. "I was wondering if you'd come shopping with me today."

"Good God no," he said through a mouthful of toast. "I hate shopping."

"But how do you get your stuff if you don't go shopping?" She waved vaguely round the kitchen.

"I buy it all on line."

"What, even your clothes?"

"My father makes all my clothes," Richard said. "He's a tailor."

Tracy was silent. She couldn't imagine how a millionaire could have a tailor for a father.

Her lower lip trembled. "I wanted to look at some new clothes. I hoped you'd come and help me decide."

He repressed a shudder, remembering the dreadful whore's dress she had turned up in for their first date.

"I'd be no good for that," he said. "I know nothing about women's clothes."

That wasn't strictly true. He learnt a lot from Chrissie, who had impeccable taste in clothes and could wear dramatic things without ever looking flashy. He sighed. It was nearly a year now and still every night he hoped she would come back.

"Can't you get one of your girlfriends to go?"

The lip trembled a little more. "I wanted you to come because I wanted to buy stuff you liked. Please."

The last word came out almost in a whisper.

Richard sighed again and stood up from the table.

"All right then. I'll just tidy up in here while you get dressed."

Twenty minutes later Tracy staggered out of the bathroom, make-up repaired, wearing the red dress and the six-inch heels. Richard winced and led the way out of the apartment. Please God they weren't going anywhere where he'd see people he knew. Maybe he could buy her something, he mused. Soften the blow.

She took him to an area of Manchester he'd never seen before; to what was clearly a very up-market centre, and marched him into a shop with the improbable name of *Flashers*. He decided it must be the name of some obscure fashion house.

There was only one item in the window. It seemed to be comprised mainly of feathers in a particularly virulent shade of purple. He couldn't even identify what sort of a garment it was supposed to be. Perhaps Tracy had got it wrong and this was a costume hire shop.

That idea was dispelled as soon as they entered. It looked nothing like a shop at all. There was no counter, just several settees with various pot plants and coffee tables scattered about. It looked, in fact, rather like he imagined the ante room to a brothel would look.

Three assistants, all horribly thin, all with bleached blonde hair, came out in a kind of controlled rush. He got the impression they were all trying to get to him first without appearing to be pushy. The first one to reach him stretched out her hand and said, rather breathlessly, "Good morning, Sir. How can I help you?" The other two ground to a halt behind her and scowled.

Richard stared back at her, nonplussed. Did he really look as if he were the customer here? He waved his hand towards Tracy, who had perched herself on the edge of one of the sofas and was leaning forward with an expression of suppressed excitement.

"Ah, it is for Madame," said the assistant, taking Tracy's hand. "What did you have in mind?"

"Well, I thought I'd like to look at something dressy for the evening," Tracy said, all girlish excitement.

Richard suppressed another shudder. He was about to pick up one of the magazines lying on the nearest coffee table when a second assistant came over. *Where are all the customers?* he wondered. *Surely we can't be the only people in the shop.*

"Can I offer you a cup of tea or coffee while you wait?" she asked.

"Coffee please." She scuttled off, wobbling dangerously on heels even higher than Tracy's. He could never understand why women wore instruments of torture. It wasn't even as if they looked good. Chrissie used to wear much lower heels – kitten heels, she called them. Consequently, rather than tottering about like a drunkard, she was able to walk with a kind of elegant grace that people like Tracy would never achieve. Such a rush of longing for Chrissie swept over him that he rocked slightly. *Jesus!* After all this time it was still as painful and immediate as when she first went away.

The assistant appeared shortly afterwards with a tray containing not only coffee but a plate of biscuits and, unbelievably, a small vase of flowers. She placed this carefully on the coffee table and withdrew, wobbling on her spindly heels. He looked at the offering with a measure of trepidation. The cup was very delicate, probably bone china, with one of those handles that was just slightly too small to admit a finger. Carefully he pinched the handle between finger and thumb and conveyed the cup to his mouth. The coffee wasn't bad actually, filter rather than espresso, but at least it wasn't instant. This sort of thing always made him feel uncomfortable. He was a big man, not fat, but very wide and very tall. This scenario was a little too like the bull in the china shop for comfort.

He sipped at the coffee daintily, that being the only way to approach such a cup, and tried to read the magazine at the same time. It appeared to consist entirely of articles about clothes, make-up, jewellery, etc. which he supposed was reasonable for a clothes shop.

He'd managed to finish the coffee and had just begun reading an article about some celebrity he'd never heard of who had turned up to some awards ceremony he had never heard of wearing an 'original' by a designer he had never heard of. He was about to turn the page when Tracy re-entered surrounded by the three assistants who were fluttering and tweeting like birds.

He gasped. Tracy was wearing an outfit – well, he supposed it was a dress - in bright orange. The bodice was fitted to the waist, then flared out alarmingly to just above knee-length where it was gathered in tightly. He couldn't decide whether it actually restricted her movement or whether the high heels were beginning to take their toll. He hadn't noticed until now just how thin and white her legs were. She looked like a famine victim wearing a beach ball.

"What do you think?"

"Très élégante," one of the assistants murmured. "And only one thousand, nine hundred guineas."

Richard, who had been about to comment on how hideous the outfit was, was momentarily lost for words.

"Can I have it?" Tracy asked.

Richard transferred his attention from the assistant.

"Tracy," he said quietly, "you look like a pumpkin on stilts. But if you want to pay two thousand pounds for a dress, that's your business. Just don't expect me to walk down the street with you wearing it."

The three assistants drew back in unison with an indrawn hissing breath, reminding him irresistibly of a nest of vipers.

"You expect *me* to pay for it?" Tracy whispered.

"I don't expect anyone to pay for it. Nobody in their right mind would pay for it. But it's your money."

"Richard," she whispered back. "You know I haven't got that kind of money."

"Then why," he said, his voice rising as he spoke, "did you bring me to this appalling place."

"Richard," Tracy tried once more, "you're embarrassing me."

"What?" his voice rose to a shout. The three assistants shrank back. "*I'm* embarrassing *you!* Don't talk to me about embarrassment. I have never been so embarrassed in my whole life. You brought me here" – he broke off when he saw the assistants watching him avidly, their eyes shiny. "I'll see you outside," he said and marched through the door.

On the way out the front cover of a magazine caught his eye but it was hardly the moment to stop and browse, so he carried on walking, his brow creased in a frown.

The shop, salon, whatever it was, faced onto a small square with trees and wooden benches. He sat down in a shady spot facing the doorway and awaited her return. This seemed to be the ideal moment to finish it for good. He was so angry he didn't suppose for one moment that he would find it difficult.

Ten minutes later Tracy came flying out of the doorway, dressed once more in the red dress, which actually looked quite tasteful after the pumpkin, and teetered on the step, looking round. She spotted him and came marching up, only tottering slightly.

"You bastard!" she shouted.

The few shoppers in the square stopped in their tracks and turned their eyes towards this unexpected source of entertainment.

"How could you do that to me?" Without waiting for an answer she carried on. "For a millionaire you are the meanest, tightest, most miserable bastard I've ever met." At the word 'millionaire' the interest of the shoppers peaked even more. "And," she said, delivering the deadliest blow she could think of, "you are crap in bed."

At least, Richard thought, *I don't scream like a fish wife in the middle of the street.*

But he said nothing; just continued to stare at her.

"Fuck you!" She turned and stamped out of the square, her departure only slightly marred by tripping over a cobblestone and doing a small wobble and skip to retain her balance.

I don't know how she can walk in them at all," he thought, shaking his head.

The shoppers were all glaring at him as if he were some kind of monster.

All except one. A girl with dark blonde hair who stood in a doorway on the other side of the square, her eyes shiny with unshed tears.

Christine

Christine woke up in a white room. There were tubes coming out of machines attached to various parts of her anatomy. She stretched out her arm. It was painfully thin and white, with a needle sticking in it. She tried to sit up, but felt too weak to make the effort. A voice said, "She's come round. She's awake." She heard the sound of rubber soles tapping on tiles as someone walked out of the room and down a corridor. The owner of the voice put a hand under her neck and helped her to rise up a little in the bed. It was a young woman in a nurse's uniform, her blond hair tied back under a little cap.

She was suddenly gripped with panic. What was she doing here? Was it the anorexia? Had she gone over some boundary that made them admit her to hospital? "My husband," she croaked, her voice a thin, rusty thread.

"It's all right." The nurse smiled. "He'll be here soon. They're just contacting him now. He's been very concerned about you."

Christine gave a nod and lay back gratefully among the pillows. She could sleep now she knew Ricky was on his way.

But the man who turned up was the wrong husband.

At first she didn't recognise the thin little man sitting at the side of the bed.

She had no idea who he was until he spoke, and then she realised with something like amazement that it was Kevin. She didn't remember him being this thin and white and, well, insipid. She was so disappointed she could hardly speak. Instead she lay back against the pillows and tried to make sense of what was going on.

A long time ago it seemed to her the nondescript little man at the side of the bed had hurt her so badly that she had decided to kill herself. She believed that they had loved each other. She had thought they were special. But then she found out he was having an affair with a woman called Daphne. He didn't think it mattered. He thought she was being unreasonable. So she had taken all the pills and drunk all the alcohol in the house and waited to die.

But instead of dying she woke up in a different life – a life where she had never met Kevin, never gone to university, never had any children. She had instead defied her parents and gone into modelling. And God was she good at it! Her face was on the front page of all the magazines. She became very rich. She became a celebrity. She fell in love with and married a millionaire. She was utterly, blissfully happy.

There was only one fly in the ointment. She missed her children with a fierce pain that refused to die away. The children that didn't exist in that life. As far as she knew she had no way of getting them back. And so, having no choice, she endured the pain.

It should be Ricky sitting at the side of her bed. He would put his arm around her and tell her everything was all right. And it would be. She looked across with something approaching disdain at the poor excuse for a man who was sitting there instead. Having experienced real love she saw what she had felt for Kevin as the shallow thing it was.

The little man at the side of the bed was speaking, "Christine," he said. "Darling. I've been so worried."

"What do you want?" she whispered.

His face took on a sad expression. "Darling, I just want to know you're all right. Sweetheart, I need you to get better and come home."

She stared at him in disbelief. "What about Daphne?"

He shrugged. "Oh that didn't mean anything. It was just a phase."

She continued to stare and he smiled his little boy smile, the one that used to make her heart turn over. "I need you to come home, Christine. I can't manage without you."

When she didn't reply, he went on. "You know I'm useless at keeping the show on the road. I haven't managed to pay the rent for the last six weeks."

Using all the strength at her command, she raised herself up in the bed. She looked at this man whom she used to love. This man who had fathered her children. For eight years she had cleaned his house, laundered his clothes, cooked his meals and gone out to work to support him. And in return he had betrayed her with the pathetic Daphne, and maybe Daphne wasn't the first – *probably* she wasn't the first.

She had all the words ready. *Daphne might not mean anything to you, but she bloody well meant something to me. She destroyed me.* But it was too hard and her throat was too sore, so she just said, "Watch my lips, Kevin." And then, eyes blazing, she spat out, "FUCK OFF!"

Kevin backed off in surprise, made a half-hearted attempt at another little boy smile, then turned and walked quickly out of the room.

Christine lay back against the pillows again with a sigh. For a few minutes she was too shocked to think properly. The sight of Kevin had completely unnerved her. All she wanted was Ricky's comforting arm around her. But was there a Ricky? There was a real possibility that he didn't exist, that her life with him had been some kind of a dream. No, she couldn't believe that. It hadn't felt like a dream. It felt like she had woken up in another life – a life where she was loved and cherished by a husband very different from the one she had just thrown out of the room. *Oh God, if there is a God, please let him exist in this life.*

Of course the most rational explanation was that he was a dream conjured up by her subconscious to console her. Think about it. All the things she'd wanted were in it – success, fame, wealth and love. Only one thing was missing – her children. In the 'dream' she had longed for her children. And then there was the anorexia. Why would she introduce that if she was trying to comfort herself?

If, however, she had visited some sort of alternative universe – a parallel life – he *must* exist in this one too, because up to the age of sixteen or so her memories in the two time streams were identical. So he would already have been born and aged about

eighteen at the point where time divided. She needed
to get onto the internet. He was a wealthy man, he
should be findable. She found she was twisting the
wedding ring on her finger. It was loose now that she
had lost so much weight. It wasn't a real wedding
ring, anyway. Kevin would never have committed
himself to a proper, legal marriage. They had gone
through some bizarre hippy ceremony in the
commune they lived in at the time. She had bought
the ring herself from Woolworths because, despite
Kevin's assurances that they didn't need a piece of
paper, that it was their vows to each other that
mattered, at heart, she was an old-fashioned girl and
believed in the conventions. She turned it round and
looked at the underside. It was tarnished. *Like my
'marriage',* she thought bitterly. With a sudden surge
of disgust she pulled it off and threw it across the
room.

    Perhaps, she thought, *I can find out about
Ricky.*"

    She had just decided she would ask the nurse
if there was a computer she could use when the door
opened and her mother came in.

    "Christine?"

    "Mum!" Christine opened her arms and her
mother rushed forward and gave her a clumsy hug,
careful to avoid all the tubes and wires.

    "Oh, love," she said, "You're awake! We
thought we'd lost you."

    To Christine's horror, her mother burst into
tears. She had only seen her mother cry once before,
when their beloved dog Patch was run over.

She gave her mother a feeble hug in return. She couldn't cry herself. She felt like a dried-out husk.

Her mother sat back and took Christine's face in her hands. "Let me look at you," she said, seemingly oblivious to the tears still running down her cheeks.

Christine reached for the cup of water on her bedside table but the wires and tubes got in the way. Her mother realised what she wanted and passed it to her. She took a deep gulp and then began to cough and splutter.

"Oh my God!" her mother said. "Nurse!"

The blonde nurse came running in, her heels slapping on the tiles.

"It's all right," she said, putting her arm under Christine's neck and helping her take another drink. "Here, darling, just take your time."

Christine gave her a grateful look and drank a little more. Then she waved at all the tubes and wires getting in her way. "Can we get rid of all this stuff? I feel like a robot."

The nurse laughed. "I'll have a word with the doctor," she said. "Now just take it easy."

She turned to Christine's mum. "She'll be dehydrated. You can refill the cup from the machine in the corridor. Don't let her drink too fast. Just a few sips at a time. I'll be back in a minute." And she left the room.

"The children?" Christine whispered. She had left her children with her mother the day she had taken the overdose.

"It's all right, love. I've got them. I wasn't going to give them to THAT MAN."

Christine smiled. As far as she knew her mother had never been able to bring herself to say Kevin's name. He had always been THAT MAN.

"He came to see me."

Her mother's anger immediately dissipated to be replaced by anxiety. "What did he want? You're not –?"

Christine shook her head. "I told him to f – get out." She recovered herself just in time.

Instantly her mother relaxed. "Oh, love, I'm so glad. He's been nothing but misery for you." She leaned over and patted her daughter's hand. "You'll come and stay with us, won't you?"

If she could have escaped from the tubes and wires she would have flung herself at her mother and hugged her. "Oh, Mum, thank you." She patted her mother's hand in turn.

"Can I see the children? Will they let them come?"

"Of course, pet. I've been bringing them in to see you every day. I only didn't bring them today because, well. . ." She gave an awkward shrug and left whatever she had been going to say unsaid. "I've left them with Vera. I'll go and fetch them."

Vera was their next-door neighbour and her mother's dearest friend. She picked up her bag and bent over to kiss her daughter goodbye.

"Mum?" Her mother had half-risen from the chair but sat down again with a thump.

"If you see the nurse, will you ask her if there's a computer I can use?"

Her mother lifted her eyebrows in surprise. "What do you want a computer for?"

"It's just something I need to look up on the net."

Her mother continued to look surprised. Christine had never shown the least interest in computers or the internet before. She picked up her bag and rummaged in it while Christine looked on with amusement. Her mother's bag was like the Tardis. Inside, beside the usual purse, tissues and pen, she carried a complete pharmacy, books, a spare pair of socks, a cardigan – the list was endless. It now included, she noticed, a pack of disposable nappies. But surely not a computer?

"There!" her mother said triumphantly, pulling out an iPad.

"Mum!" Christine exclaimed. "You've got an iPad! I don't believe it."

"Daddy bought it me for my birthday. Do you know it can have three thousand books on it? Three thousand! Imagine that!"

Christine began to laugh and immediately regretted it. She took another sip of water.

"Anyway," her mother was saying, "you're supposed to be able to get the internet on it but I don't know how."

She frowned down at the tablet.

"Give it to me," Christine whispered, barely able to contain herself. Her mother passed it across and she fell upon it like a starving wolf and began typing furiously. Her mother watched her for a moment in disbelief. Christine had never been able to type to save her life. When had she learnt to do that?

"It's all right Mum." Christine grinned up at her. "Get the children."

Her mother started walking towards the door.

"And, Mum." Her mother stopped in her tracks and turned around. "I love you."

Then she turned back to the pad and continued her furious typing.

Richard Epstein. The search brought up pages and pages about an American lawyer. It wasn't him. She tried again, adding *real estate.* There were dozens of them. She added *Manchester* and discovered there was a Manchester in Connecticut. Feeling slightly hysterical she added *England.* And there he was! With a small sob, she accessed the website *for R. Epstein, Real Estate and Property Management.* There was a photograph of his office in Piccadilly. It was the same one! The one he had when she first met him in the other life. In the flipside. She skimmed through the web page. It showed more photographs, mostly of properties for sale or rent. Seething with frustration, she clicked on *About us.* It listed all the various services available. But there, right at the bottom was *The Team.* She clicked – and there he was. She gazed at his smiling face and the *need* for him struck her like a blow, so forcefully that she uttered a hoarse sob and bent over as hot tears started to her eyes.

The blonde nurse came running in. "Are you all right?"

"Sorry," Christine said, "I'm just missing my children. That's all."

She swiped the page so the nurse wouldn't see that she was actually looking at a picture of a man.

"Your mum's bringing them in after lunch," the nurse said, "and in the meantime, I'm going to get rid of all these tubes and wires. I'll just leave the catheter until we're sure you can make it to the bathroom on your own."

Catheter! Bloody hell! Christine shifted uncomfortably on the bed. She couldn't feel anything untoward down there.

The nurse finished removing the tubes. Her arm bled slightly where a needle had been pulled out but it didn't hurt. She flexed her arms and stretched. "God, that feels good."

"Would you like to wash your face and hands?"

"Oh, please." She hadn't realised how grubby she felt. "And can I brush my teeth? My mouth tastes awful."

The nurse laughed. "I'll get you a brush and some toothpaste. And I can wash your hair for you if you like."

Christine could have kissed her.

Afterwards she pulled out the iPad again and just gazed at Ricky's face. *How on earth,* she wondered, *am I going to get him back?*

Lunch was vile. Some kind of unidentifiable meat, minced up, the kind of mashed potatoes you use to get for school dinners; horrible, overcooked, tasteless greens. It was a bit sad for her first meal (in this life anyway) for three months. She picked at it and pushed it around her plate. While she did so she thought about Ricky and how difficult it was going to be to get him back. She couldn't just walk up to him and say, "Hey, Ricky, it's me!" As far as he was concerned he had never seen her before in his life. And, let's be honest here, she wasn't exactly a catch. A university drop-out with two children. He had said once that if they couldn't have their own children they could adopt, but that was different, wasn't it? Different from taking on two children your lover had conceived with another man, a constant reminder that she had once loved someone else. And then there was perhaps the most insurmountable problem of all – he was a millionaire and she was completely penniless. Until the overdose she had been working nights in a bacon factory. Fine catch she was! At best she would look like a gold digger and at worst some kind of crazed stalker.

There was one little gleam of sunshine, though. No mention in his, admittedly brief, biography of a wife. She should have looked him up on Wikipedia. She was just reaching for the iPad when a woman came in and took away her dinner tray. "Not hungry, love?" she asked, looking disapprovingly at the almost untouched offering.

Christine shook her head and reached once again for the iPad. The door opened again and a doctor came in. At least, she assumed he was a doctor. He was in a white coat. But he looked awfully young. He smiled at her and sat on the end of the bed. "So, our sleeping beauty has woken up," he said. "Were you kissed by a prince?"

"Yes," said Christine, thinking of last night, when she and Ricky had made love, not knowing it was for the last time.

The doctor, if he was a doctor, laughed and held out his hand. "I'm Dr Newton," he said. So he *was* a real doctor. "I just want to run a few tests and if the results are all satisfactory we can let you go home tomorrow."

Christine's face fell. "Can't I go home today?"

Still smiling, he shook his head. "I'm afraid not. We won't have all the results till mid-morning at the earliest."

Christine swallowed her disappointment and smiled back. After all, it wasn't *his* fault.

When they trundled her back from the CAT scan she found her father waiting outside her room. "Daddy!"

He looked up with such joy that it brought tears to her eyes.

"Darling!"

He followed her into the room and sat in the plastic chair beside her.

"Christine!" He hugged her with such ferocity that she thought her ribs might crack. "I didn't believe it when your mother rang. I couldn't believe you'd woken up at last. We thought we'd lost you. We thought . . . they said . . ." His voice tailed away.

"*What* did they say?"

"They said you would probably never wake up. They said that if you did you might be a vegetable. They said –" his voice cracked. "They said we should be thinking about switching off the life support. And, God forgive me, I was considering it." The last words trembled on the edge of a scream.

"Of course you were, Daddy. Anyone would. It was the right thing to do."

"Your mum wouldn't have. She would have fought tooth and nail to keep you going."

Christine laughed. She could imagine her mother standing by the bed, ready to kick anyone in the balls who tried to switch her off. "Yes, she would. But it still wouldn't necessarily have been the right decision. Anyway, Ricky says guilt is a useless emotion. It makes you miserable and it doesn't help the person you feel guilty about."

"I suppose you're right," her dad said but he still looked miserable. "Who's Ricky?"

"I'll tell you all about it, Daddy," Christine said, leaning forward. But they were interrupted as the door opened and a small child shot across the room and landed on the bed with such force that it shook.

"Hey, steady on," said her father, whilst her mother, from the doorway, said, "I'm sorry. He got away from me."

She was holding baby James in one arm, her handbag dangling from the other.

"Mummy," said Timmy, scaling her as if she were a minor mountain, "you've been asleep for *ages*. I *missed* you."

"I missed you too," she said, holding him to her, smelling his clean, little boy smell.

"What, when you were asleep?"

"I missed you in my sleep."

Her mother stood by the bed, holding out baby James who was regarding her with an astonished, slightly horrified expression.

"He doesn't remember me!" she cried, devastated. But then the baby smiled and held out his arms to her.

Christine held her children and felt as if a great gaping hole in her life had been filled. She was almost completely happy. Almost.

When it was time for them to go, she wept uncontrollably. "I can't bear it. Not again!"

Her parents exchanged a look. *Again?* What did she mean?

"Don't take them away!"

"But, darling, you'll see them in the morning," her mother said, gently prising the baby from her grip.

"Daddy," Christine said. "You've got to get me out of here. The food's *awful*."

Her father laughed and ruffled her hair as if she were a small child.

"You'll live," he said, gave her a brief hug and stood up.

"Oh, I almost forgot," he said, reaching into his briefcase. "I've got something for you." He pulled out another iPad. Christine's eyes widened in surprise. "Your mother couldn't possibly manage till tomorrow without hers." He passed it over. "I've registered it with my Amazon account, so you can download anything your mother's already bought." He laughed at Christine's disgusted expression. Her mother's taste in literature was firmly centred on

Mills and Boon. "And," he went on, "you can get anything else you fancy with one-click." He watched her closely to see whether she knew what one-click was. She clearly did.

"Daddy, I can't possibly buy stuff on your account. What do you take me for?"

"My beautiful daughter, back from dead. Well, the unconscious, anyway. And don't worry it's hardly going to break the bank. We can talk about it later. Meantime, enjoy. And give me back your mother's before I forget."

She handed it over and kissed him goodbye.

But after he had gone, she didn't download any books. She just stared at the picture of Ricky.

It was a long night. Dinner arrived and was even more disgusting than lunch. She pushed it around her plate, wondering why hospital food was so bad. Surely they could do better. You'd think they'd be concerned about keeping up the patients' morale. She wondered how many people died because the horrible food made them lose the will to live.

They took away her tray and she lay back and tried to relax. She was torn between fear of going to sleep in case she slipped straight back into the flipside and a terrible desire to see Ricky again, hold him again. Only the thought of losing her children kept her from trying to throw herself back into that other world. Eventually she slept anyway and if she dreamed she didn't remember.

But while she slept the little men in the basement of her mind were beavering away, working on the problem of how to get Ricky back; and when she awoke she had the answer. She would do it all again – everything she had done on the flipside. She would once again become an internationally known model. Why not? She knew she could do it. She'd done it before. The only problem was she would need some money to get started.

Breakfast arrived – a tepid cup of tea and two slices of slightly warmed, but not actually toasted, bread, accompanied by three little foil containers containing UHT milk, butter and the kind of jam that just tastes of sugar and seems to have had no acquaintance whatsoever with the fruit it purported to be made from.

She was so hungry that she ate it anyway. And she drank the tea, even though she was desperate for coffee. Ah well! She reached for the iPad and accessed the picture of Ricky again. I'll find you, she promised the smiling photo. I'll get you back.

The door opened and her father came in, carrying a large carrier bag.

"Hi, Darling," he said.

"Daddy, aren't you working today?"

"I've taken a couple of days off," he said. "It isn't every day you get your favourite daughter back."

"Daddy!" she said, laughing. "I'm your only daughter."

"And my favourite." He kissed her on the cheek and opened the carrier bag. "I wasn't sure what you'd want, so I got a selection."

He passed her a bacon sandwich. She snatched it from him and took a huge bite. "Oh God, that's so wonderful," she said, through a mouthful of bread. Her father grinned and went on to produce an egg sandwich, a packet of crisps, two hash browns, a croissant and, Oh joy! A large cup of McDonald's coffee.

"Oh, Daddy, you're a saviour," she said between sips. It was hot and strong and utterly wonderful. "I love you so much."

"Now," he said, "tell me about Ricky."

And she did. She told him everything, how she had woken up in an alternative life, the flipside. How in that other life she had been a successful model. How she had met and married the love of her life.

"I thought Kevin was the love of your life."

"So did I until I found out what real love is like."

"Well," said her father, "I must say all this is a great relief to me."

"So you believe me?"

He thought about that for a moment. "The obvious explanation is that you dreamt it," he said, "but I don't think that works."

Christine lifted her eyebrows.

"Your brain activity during the coma argues against it. The reason they thought you would never recover was that there was no evidence of dreaming. Your brain appeared to be dead for all except basic body functions. No rapid eye movement. No electrical activity signalling thought. Nothing to suggest anything intelligent was going on at all. It was as if your mind, your soul, whatever you want to call it, had departed. Which was why. . ." his voice tailed off and he gave a shrug. He cleared his throat.

"Anyway, I think I've read something along those lines."

Christine sat forward, all her attention on her father. "What? What lines?"

"Well, it was something about there being an infinite number of dimensions, all existing in the same space." He shook his head. "Sorry, I can't remember any more. I'll have to look it up."

At that moment the young doctor walked in. "What's all this?" he asked, looking at the sandwich wrappings on the bed. Christine guiltily swept them up and stuffed them in the carrier bag. "Sorry, but I was starving."

He lifted an eyebrow. "Didn't they feed you?"

"Yes but it was awful. I couldn't eat it."

Doctor Newton burst out laughing. "Nothing wrong with your appetite anyway."

"Is there anything wrong with anything else?"

The doctor turned to Christine's father and shook his hand. "Hello, Mr Jones. No, as far as we can tell, she's in tip-top condition, apart from some muscle wastage. All the tests checked out." He turned to Christine. "I'm booking you in for physiotherapy for two weeks."

Christine was aghast. "TWO WEEKS? But I want to go home."

The doctor laughed again. "You can go home straight away. You attend physiotherapy as an outpatient."

Christine heaved an enormous sigh of relief. "Right," she said. "Where are my clothes?"

~ * ~

Her parents were wonderful. Her mother drove her to physiotherapy and back every day and her father offered to take her to her old house to pick up her stuff. After a moment's hesitation, her mother said she would come too and the three of them set off, leaving the boys with Vera.

As it turned out, all Christine's fears about meeting Kevin were unfounded. He was nowhere in evidence. When they got there, the house had an abandoned, unfriendly look. She let herself in with her key and drew back in shock at the state of the place. Her lovely, tidy house was in chaos; there were takeaway packages all over the living room floor, cups scattered everywhere, some with green mould in them, and the kitchen sink was piled high with washing up. There was a faint, unsavoury smell of unwashed clothes and stale food. She could have cried.

Her mother came in behind her, wrinkling her nose at the smell and the squalor.

"Ugh!" she said.

But the children's room was just as she left it; the boys' clothes neatly hung in the wardrobe; the drawers full of neatly folded clean clothes; and all around the room toys and books sat tidily on the shelves.

"I'll deal with these," said her father, entering the room carrying a large plastic bin bag. Christine and her mother went to deal with the holocaust in the kitchen.

"Well, he's not keeping this." Her mother pulled down the slow cooker from the shelf, wrapped it in a none-too-clean towel and put it in her own bin bag.

Christine concealed a smile. Her mother had bought the slow cooker for her; had insisted even though Christine had protested that she'd rather have the money (Timmy desperately needed new shoes). But her mother had gone ahead and bought the cooker anyway. Christine had used it once, thought the casserole had an unpleasant chemical taste and had never used it again. Since all the crockery was filthy and she didn't like it much anyway, she decided to abandon it.

The living room was in an unholy mess but she pressed her lips together and retrieved her favourite books and a couple of cushions her grandmother had made. Now there only remained her clothes.

"What about the bedding?" her mother asked.

Christine shook her head. "I don't know who's been sleeping in it."

Without pausing to sort through, she swept all her clothes into the bag,

"OK, let's go."

As she left the house she felt a great swelling relief. It was over. She had left all the mess behind. Time to get on with her real life.

~ * ~

That evening she talked to her parents about Ricky. Her father, of course, already knew but her mother looked decidedly worried.

"I know what you're thinking, Mum. You think I dreamt it but I didn't. Ricky is real. He exists here in this life. I found him on the internet. Look!"

She opened her iPad and showed her mother the photograph.

"Isn't he gorgeous?"

"Yes but," her mother said, flapping her hand in a vague, distracted gesture, "don't you think you might have just come across him before and incorporated him in your dream?"

"Mum, am I likely to consort with millionaires?"

"Well, I didn't mean you'd actually met him. Just seen him on the news or something."

Her father patted her mother's hand. "Let her tell you about it."

Her mother subsided but her hands fidgeted in her lap as they always did when she was anxious.

"The thing is," Christine said. "I need to borrow some money."

Neither of them said anything.

She explained her plan, miserably aware that it sounded ridiculous as soon as she said it out loud. "I'll pay you back. I promise. I know I can do it. I just need some money to get started."

"How much do you need?" her father asked gently.

"I think I could do it for a thousand pounds, definitely for two thousand. I know it's a lot to ask but –"

"Tell her, Beryl."

Her mother shot an angry look at her father.

"It's a mad scheme," she said. "She'll just lose the money and be disappointed."

"Honestly, Mum, I can do it. I did it before."

Her mother snorted. "In a dream."

"I don't believe it was a dream," her father said. "I think she did travel to another dimension. I've looked it up. It's a perfectly respectable scientific theory."

"But—"

He put his finger over her lips. "It doesn't matter," he said. "It doesn't matter whether it was a dream or if it was real. It's what she wants to do. It will make her happy."

Christine shot him a look of pure gratitude.

Her mother gave a little grimace.

"And we stopped her before. It was all she ever wanted to do and we persuaded her to go to university instead. And look how that turned out! Tell her."

Her mother cleared her throat then in a slightly strangled voice said, "You don't need to borrow any money. We've got a trust fund for you. We started it when you were born and we've been adding to it ever since. We thought . . . we thought it would be enough for a deposit on a house but what with house prices going up and interest rates going down it won't be near enough." There were tears in her mother's eyes now. "I didn't tell you because I didn't want you to give it to THAT MAN."

A tiny, mean part of Christine felt a sudden surge of anger but she suppressed it.

"How much is it?" she whispered.

"It was more than twenty thousand last time I checked but that was ages ago."

"What?"

Her father was laughing. "Will it be enough, do you think?"

"Oh, Daddy. I don't believe it. It's wonderful. You're wonderful. Both of you."

And if she thought about the times she had struggled to pay the rent or the electricity bills, she pushed the thought away and got up to hug her parents.

~ * ~

Two months later she stood naked in front of her bedroom mirror eying her reflection dispassionately. She had exercised religiously, not just for the two weeks of physiotherapy but at home twice a day ever since. Now she had all her muscle tone back. She was slim and shapely and as good as she was ever going to get.

It was time.

Having agreed to go along with it, her mother threw herself into the endeavour with great enthusiasm. They went off shopping together day after day, arm-in-arm, looking for just the right outfits. This was what she had always imagined her relationship with her mother would be like, before the dreadful rows over university and the advent of the appalling Kevin. They were good friends again.

When she had finally amassed a good collection, she put on a fashion show for her parents and the boys. Her father played his favourite albums while Christine paraded up and down the living room, in one outfit after another. Her father looked bemused, her mother excited, the boys laughed.

The next day she booked an appointment with Jason Wade, the top fashion photographer. She wondered whether he would remember her. She had been to school with Jason. He was mad about photography even then and she was mad about fashion. They had fantasised about working together when they grew up; she a top model, he a top photographer, but she had given up on her dreams, gone off to be a student and met the vile Kevin. She couldn't remember the last time she had spoken to Jason. Maybe not during the whole ten years since they left school. She had been really pleased to find him on the net, although, to her surprise, he had a studio in Manchester, not the Mayfair studio he had in the flipside. Perhaps he hadn't been quite so successful in this time stream. But that didn't matter. He was still the best.

She packed all her new clothes into two suitcases, made herself up with care, and took a taxi to Jason's studio. It was considerably more modest than his flipside Mayfair property, but nevertheless it had style. It exuded class. She opened the door and went in. The girl behind the counter smiled at her. "Miss J?" she asked.

Christine smiled back. "Yes," she said, putting down the suitcases.

"Here, let me help you with those." The girl picked one up and led the way through to the back. Jason was just coming out, wearing a professional smile. It faltered slightly as he saw her and a small frown appeared between his eyebrows. "Have we met before?"

"Oh, Jason, it's me. We were at school together."

"Bugger me," said Jason, dropping all pretence of professionalism. "It's Christine Jones." He enveloped her in a bear hug. "Come through, you'll love it. I can't believe it. After all this time. What happened to you? You look bloody marvellous."

Laughing, she followed him into the studio, telling him as she went about the deviation from her original plans. "But I'm back on track now," she finished, "and all I need is a portfolio. I want the absolutely, most stunning, fabulous portfolio you can put together."

"Well, you're certainly giving me good material to work with. Let's have a look at your gear."

One by one Christine pulled out her garments, lining them up, each with its own accessories, and they discussed backgrounds and lighting for each.

"How many days will it take?" she asked.

"Oh, I think we can do it in one."

"One! I thought it would take at least three."

"Digital camera," said Jason, grinning. "It takes me more time to set up the shot than to actually do it." He held up his camera and kissed it. "I was sceptical at first but now I think it's the best thing that ever happened. So quick. No waste. I can see exactly what I've got and I don't have to take a hundred shots to get the one I want."

Things seemed to have progressed rather faster here than in the flipside. She remembered digital cameras coming out but only a year or so ago and she had given up modelling soon after because of the anorexia.

They worked happily together for most of the morning, only stopping for one short break, and Christine realised that they would indeed finish in one day.

Jason got more and more excited as the day progressed. "That's great," he shouted. "Hold that. God these are going to be good. Turn a bit to the left. Wow, that's fabulous."

How on earth had she let a good friend like Jason slip through her fingers, Christine wondered, and she suddenly realised that she had lost all her friends, not just Jason but all her schoolmates and her friends from college. The knowledge came as a revelation. Kevin had done it. He had isolated her, put her friends off. Kept her to himself. She frowned and Jason went into ecstasies. "Hold that frown! You look so disdainful! God, that's brilliant. You're a natural."

The office girl brought them sandwiches for lunch and then they carried on for another couple of hours.

"Last one," Christine said. Her legs were beginning to ache from standing still but she was nowhere near as exhausted as she used to get in the flipside. Mind you, she wasn't suffering from anorexia here.

Together they looked through the pictures. "These are very good," Christine said.

"Good! They're brilliant! They're going to make us famous. We're going to do it, Christine Jones." And he grabbed her and swung her into an impromptu dance. The office girl appeared in the doorway and stood uncertainly watching them. "Am I all right to shut up shop?" she asked. Feeling slightly embarrassed, Christine stopped dancing and sat down while Jason and the girl discussed appointments made that day. The girl was standing a little too close to him, their shoulders touching, occasionally shooting a slightly resentful glance in Christine's direction.

She's on a sticky wicket there, Christine thought. Jason is as gay as old Paree.

Her taxi arrived, Jason carried her suitcases over, the driver put them in the boot and Christine climbed in the back. Jason leaned over and kissed her goodbye through the window. "I'll email you the pictures and you choose which ones you want in the portfolio." He grinned with sheer delight. "But it won't be easy. They're all shit hot."

Christine laughed aloud and waved goodbye to the girl, who managed a small smile and waved back.

She was so flushed with the success of the shoot that she was paying no attention to her surroundings, so when the taxi ground to a halt at the traffic lights it came as a complete surprise to discover that she was looking straight at Ricky's office on the other side of the square. R. Epstein, Real Estate and Property Management. As she watched, the door opened and Ricky himself walked out. She gave a small cry, half gasp of surprise, half sob. The taxi driver looked over his shoulder. "Are you all right, luv?"

She nodded. "Sorry. I just saw somebody I know. It was a surprise."

"Do you want me to park up?"

"No," she said, not taking her eyes off Ricky, "no, that's OK."

The lights changed and the taxi started off. Christine turned in her seat and watched Ricky until he was out of sight. Then she turned back to face the front, her eyes full of unshed tears.

Later that evening the taxi driver would tell his wife about the beautiful young woman he had picked up from the studio. "She were so bonny and she were so sad."

"Sounds like you fancied her," his wife said with an arch smile.

"No. . . I wouldn't ever . . ." he said, confused. Then he realised she was laughing at him and he grabbed her and sat her on his knee. "I've got me hands full at home."

~ * ~

Two weeks later Christine was sitting in Angela Dekker's waiting room clutching her portfolio and glancing from time to time at the receptionist as she waited to be ushered in to the august presence of the great agent. This was going to be tricky. For the first time she was meeting someone she had never met before in this life but who was a very good friend in the flipside. She was going to have to tread very carefully. It would be so easy to offend her with over-familiarity. A buzzer sounded and the receptionist looked over with a smile. "You can go in now," she said.

Angela was on the phone when Christine entered. Unsure whether it would be all right to sit down, she wandered about the room looking at the photographs of famous models.

"That's Carla May," a voice said at her shoulder. She had been staring at the poster of the stunning brunette and hadn't heard the phone call come to an end or Angela get up from her desk.

"I know," Christine said, turning to face her. "She's gorgeous, isn't she."

Angela smiled. Then her brow creased in a faint frown. "Have we met before?"

Christine was taken aback. They couldn't have done, could they? Was there somehow an affinity between people who had met on the flipside?

"Perhaps we go to the same parties," she suggested.

"Hmm," she said unconvinced." Come and sit down and I'll have a look at your portfolio. Would you like a cup of tea? Or coffee?"

"Coffee please," said Christine and continued her inspection of the portraits on the wall whilst Angela ordered the drinks and then paid attention to the portfolio. Jason had done a magnificent job. The front page was a dramatic photograph of her wearing an enormous hat, her face partially in shade. Running across the page in an upward diagonal was her professional name, Chrystal J.

"Nice," Angela muttered. She began to flick through the rest. Christine sipped her coffee.

Angela looked up. "These are very good," she said. "Who did them?"

"Jason Wade," Christine said, leaning across to look at the open page. "He's brilliant. I always use him."

Angela frowned. "How come I've not come across you before? Where have you been working?"

"I haven't been working for a while. I stopped modelling when I married." She had nearly said, 'and had children' but got confused. She had married in one life and had children in the other.

Angela shook her head. "So why return now?"

Christine breathed an inner sigh of relief. For the time being she had avoided more awkward questions about where she had worked. She'd rather not claim things which, although true in the flipside, couldn't be proved in this time stream.

"My marriage broke up. I decided to do what I like best."

A brief smile from Angela. "Well if these are a sample I don't think we'll have any trouble finding you work. Can I hang on to this?"

"Of course. It's not the only copy." Christine relaxed and smiled at her new agent.

"I still can't remember where we met," Angela said. "It's really annoying me."

Christine smiled to herself. *If I told you you'd think I was bonkers*, she thought.

"I'll get Lucy to type up a contract." She picked up the phone and had a brief conversation, then stood up, moved round the desk, pulled over another chair and sat beside her.

"Now, tell me all about yourself."

As soon as she got home, Christine called Jason. "I think you're likely to get some commissions from Angela Dekker." She waited for his exuberance to die down a bit, then went on. "You need to put your prices up or she won't take you seriously."

~ * ~

The next few months were a whirlwind of activity. Christine was working most days, spending her evenings with her family and in between she began following Ricky on the net. At first she was stymied because he didn't seem to have any social media accounts. A search just brought up his Wikipedia entry and posts about his business. But then she had a brainwave. She followed the Facebook and Twitter accounts of his team; and those of his friends, the ones she had met in the flipside. She found photographs. Not a lot, but something to drool over for a while.

She desperately needed to hold him. But if she couldn't do that, at least see him. Now and then, on days when she wasn't working, she sat in the cafe opposite his office and watched for him to come out. Sometimes he did. She was miserably aware that she had become a crazed stalker.

Then came the phone call from Angela. "We've got it, Chrissie. We made it! You've got a contract with Joanna Elizabeth!!!" Christine sat down with a bump. Joanna Elizabeth! The best designer in Europe. No, make that the world. And one of Christine's best friends in the flipside.

"Wow," she said. "Do I have to go to Paris?"

"No, she's in London for a show. I've got you an interview with her on Tuesday. Then I've got interviews lined up with all the big magazines. You're on your way, kid."

Christine drew a deep breath. She was nearly there. Her face would be on all the magazines. She could meet him at last.

~ * ~

Two weeks later, with her face already on a couple of the lesser magazines, she sat in the cafe watching Ricky's office. Today she was rewarded. Only he didn't come out of the office. He came out of the next door along; the one leading to his penthouse apartment. And he was not alone. The woman with him came tottering out wearing ludicrously high heels and an even more ludicrous shiny red dress. Christine's hand flew to her mouth as a red hot stab of jealousy shot through her. Without a moment's thought, she left a five pound note on the table and followed them. Ricky kept looking around him with a guilty, hunted look. Maybe she was a prostitute. She certainly dressed like one. But that didn't seem like his style at all. Could she be a client? But then, why would she have been in his private apartment?

Not my business, she thought. But she followed them anyway, through back streets, away from the centre, ending up in a small square surrounded by shops, with trees and benches in the centre. Ricky and the strange girl went into a shop oddly-named *Flashers*. Christine slid into the shadow of a shop doorway. Flashers seemed to be some sort of designer dress shop but, if the weird purple creation in the window was anything to go by, it was doomed to failure. She should go. She should just get a taxi and go home. Following him was taking the crazed stalker thing just a little too far.

But she stayed. *Just one more look*, she thought. *I just need to see him one more time and then I can wait another few weeks. I can* wait *until I'm in all the magazines.*

She waited. And eventually he came out. Alone. She had never seen him look so angry. He sat on one of the benches in the little square staring straight ahead, his face white with rage. She wanted to go to him and ask him what had happened. She wanted to soothe him. She even took a tentative step forward and then pulled herself together. What was she doing? She was about to blow the whole thing.

And then the girl came out, tottering on her high heels, looking like an angry tomato. "You bastard!" she shrieked. And then let forth a stream of abuse ending with "For a millionaire you are the meanest, tightest, most miserable bastard I've ever met. And you are crap in bed."

The shoppers in the square had all stopped to watch the free show.

Ricky did nothing. He just stared back at the girl, the only sign of his anger being a small tick at the side of his jaw.

Having delivered her final, deadly shot, the girl gave in and staggered off, tripping over a cobblestone as she went and very nearly coming to grief.

Christine wanted to run to him and throw her arms around him and tell him he was the greatest lover in the world. Instead, with a supreme effort, she slid further back into the shadows, the tears now running freely down her cheeks. The shoppers, disappointed that the show appeared to be over, went back to their shopping.

After a while Ricky stood up, brushed himself down with a rather fastidious movement, as if he were ridding himself of something unpleasant, and then, to Christine's amazement, walked straight back into the shop.

She made her escape.

Richard

The three assistants, who had been clustered around the door, avidly watching the free show outside, drew back. "He's coming back," one of them whispered. There was a soft *ching!* as the door opened and Richard entered. He gave a small start when he saw all three assistants staring at him. "Sorry," he said, "I forgot something."

He looked around for the magazine, found it and picked it up. "Jesus," he whispered, as he stared at the cover. He sat down with a bump. "Are you all right?" one of the assistants asked.

"What?" He looked up. "Yes, fine. I know her, that's all." The assistant bent to see what the picture was on the front of the magazine. "Oh my God!" she shrieked. "You know Crystal J! Oh my God! That's awesome." The other two came closer. "She is the very latest thing," one said. "Absolutely," said another. "She's just got a contract with Joanna Elizabeth. She'll be in all the rag mags next week."

Richard was once again gazing at the face on the cover. "Can I buy this?"

"Keep it," the nearest assistant said. "And don't forget to tell her about us. I think she'd like our designs, don't you, Lorelai?" Her friend tittered in reply.

Privately Richard thought the chances of Chrissie being seen dead in any of their designs were about as remote as that of the Queen taking up hang-gliding.

"Yes, of course," he said, rolling the magazine carefully into a tube and sticking it in his pocket. Then he gave a stiff little bow and left the shop.

"Funny bloke," Lorelai said. "Sexy, though," said Vanda. "And rich," added Delilah. They gave a collective sigh and gathered around the door again to watch him leave the square.

Richard didn't trust himself to look at the magazine again until he reached his apartment. There, he poured himself a beer, sat in his favourite armchair and gazed at the photograph of the woman he loved. She was real. Even the name was the same, her professional name – Crystal J. He ran his finger over the contours of the printed face, as if he could feel the living flesh. "Oh, Chrissie. I should have tried harder."

The headline read *Crystal J gains contract with Joanna Elizabeth*, then in smaller print at the bottom of the page, *See page 5 for full story*.

He turned to page 5. This consisted mainly of photographs with very little text in between. Chrissie in various outfits, some on location, some on the catwalk. The text was mainly drivel about the designs and the celebrities that wore them. He turned the page. There were more pictures. These were more informal — Chrissie as a child on a swing, laughing; Chrissie with student friends at a party; Chrissie sitting up in bed holding a new born baby.

He sat up suddenly, beer spurting out of his mouth! *Christ!* She was married! She had a child! He threw the magazine to one side, got up and went into the kitchen to wipe himself down. While he was in there he got another beer out of the fridge. Not once, not once had it crossed his mind that he would find her and she would be married to someone else. He was overwhelmed by despair.

Later he had no recollection of the rest of that day. He woke up the next morning on the settee, surrounded by empty beer cans, and with a raging headache. Feeling slightly nauseous, he staggered to the bathroom, took two Ibuprofen and drank a glass of water. Too little, too late, he feared. But it was Sunday and he had nothing to do, no-one to see.

He stripped off his rumpled clothes, dropped them in the wash basket and went to brush his teeth, have a shower and go to bed. He would sleep through the hangover.

When he got up for the second time it was early evening and he was feeling much better. There was nothing appetising in the fridge, so he picked up the phone and ordered a takeaway. As he went back into the living room, he saw the magazine lying where he had flung it, on the floor beside his chair. It was still open at the page with the baby on it. Unable to resist, he picked it up.

There is something masochistic about the desire to keep exploring the things that hurt. Like probing an aching tooth. Richard was drawn immediately to the photo of mother and child. The caption read, 'Crystal J with her eldest child, Timothy.'

Dear God Almighty. More than one child!

He resisted the urge to throw it to one side again. He had to know more. To probe the aching tooth. He read the interview in the text between the photographs, skip reading. . .

Suzanne*: So what made you decide to take up modelling?*

Chrystal J*: Well it was what I always wanted to do and so when my marriage broke up a year ago -*

"Yesss!!!" She was free. Free for him. A feeling of exultation swept over him, swiftly replaced by one of shame. She must have been dreadfully unhappy. She must have suffered. And he hadn't been there for her. Picking up the magazine he went into his study and switched on his computer. He wasn't great with computers but he knew enough to do a search on Google.

Now, what was the name of her agent? Anne something? Adrienne? Neither sounded quite right.

~ * ~

He hardly slept that night. Every so often he dropped off for a few minutes, then he woke with a start, unable to bear the wait until business hours. He had found Chrissie's agent – Angela Dekker. Now all he had to do was call her and find out where Chrissie was.

But when at last the long night was over and he finally got through to Angela's office, the receptionist wouldn't put him through.

"Miss Dekker is in a meeting at the moment, can I help you?"

"Yes, perhaps you can. I just need to know where Chrystal J is working today."

"Who is this, please?"

"My name's Richard Epstein. I'm a close friend of Miss J and I need to get in touch with her urgently."

"I'm very sorry, Mr Epstein but I really can't give away Miss J's details on the phone."

And that was that. He couldn't budge her. Eventually, defeated, he hung up.

Furious, he pulled on his jacket, ready to go to Angela Dekker's office and throttle the truth out of her, when he suddenly stopped dead in his tracks. She always worked with the same photographer, didn't she? Jason, Jason . . . he'd get it in a minute. . . WADE! That was it. He sat down at the computer again.

"Hi, is Jason there?"

"Sorry, he on a shoot today. Can I help?"

"Damn, I need to speak to him. Where is he shooting?"

"He's at that big conference centre near Heaton Park. Fashion show. Hang on, I'll get the address."

"No, don't bother," said Richard. "I know where it is."

Half an hour later the BMW screeched to a halt outside the conference centre. Richard leapt out and bounded up the steps two at a time. Half way up he met a young man in uniform coming down. "You can't park there, sir."

"Keys are in it. Move it where you like."

The man looked inclined to argue, then he saw the expression on Richard's face and the sheer size of him and thought better of it. "Right, sir," he said, but Richard had already disappeared through the front doors.

"Fashion show!" he shouted at the receptionist.

"Ballroom." She pointed to the right and Richard veered off without slowing down.

The ballroom was set up for a fashion show with a large stage at the far end, a catwalk running off it at right-angles into the audience, and rows of chairs on either side. A huge barrage of lights hung above the stage and there were some free-standing lamps at the sides. These last must have been temporary, since they were attached to wall plugs by cables running across the platform. Jason was standing off to one side with his back to the door, his camera pointed at the woman walking down the catwalk – an exceptionally beautiful woman with long, dark blonde hair.

"CHRISSIE!"

Christine stopped in mid-stride. Her eyes widened. "Ricky?" The name came out almost as a whisper. Then, "RICKY!" And she came running, heedless of the wires running across the platform. As she reached the end, she tripped over a cable and sailed off the edge, pulling one of the lamps along with her. In one balletic movement, Richard caught her in his left arm, simultaneously grabbing the lamp in his right hand.

"Wow!" said Jason. "That was brilliant! You should be on *Britain's Got Talent*. I caught it all on video." But nobody was listening to him.

Richard beamed down at Christine, who had settled into his arms with easy familiarity. "Are you all right, Poppet?"

"Ricky," she said, as if that somehow constituted an answer. She reached up and stroked his cheek. "I can't believe you're real. How did you know it was me?"

Richard guffawed and leant down to kiss her.

"So, I'll just pack up, then, shall I?" Jason asked. "Don't worry about me. Just don't forget to be here for one thirty sharp." There was no sign that either of them had heard him.

"I've got two children."

"I know."

"Doesn't it matter?"

"Why should it?"

"What about your mother?"

"My mother has been desperate for grandchildren for years."

"Yes, but —"

"Shush!"

Ricky and Chrissie

The doorbell rang and Angela went to open it.

"You can't come in," she said.

"I need to give Timmy his button-hole."

Angela turned to Chrissie. "It's Ricky."

"Oh my God! He can't see me in my dress."

"Go upstairs," hissed Joanna Elizabeth.

Chrissie fled up the stairs, her dress floating around her in the wind of her passage.

Angela opened the door.

"Timmy!" said Ricky.

The boy came forward, a big grin on his face. "Hey, Dad!"

"I'm not your dad for;" Ricky consulted his watch, "another two hours or so. Here, I've got to give you this." He knelt down to bring his face level with the boy's, took a flower from his own button-hole and carefully fixed it in that of Timmy's page-boy jacket. Timmy screwed up his face. "Flowers are for sissies."

"No, they're not. But only real men can carry off wearing them," Ricky said seriously.

"Can we do galloping horses?"

"Not now. But as soon as I'm your real dad we'll do galloping horses, and . . ." he paused dramatically, "aeroplanes."

"What is it?" Timmy's eyes were round with expectation.

"You'll see." Ricky looked over his shoulder. "Look, I've got to go. I have to be standing in the church waiting for Mummy. Now, listen. You've got a very important job. You know what to do?" Timmy nodded. "OK, then I'm leaving it in your hands. Good man."

He patted the boy on the shoulder in a manly fashion, then leant forward and gave him a bear hug.

"See you in about half an hour."

~ * ~

The church was filled to capacity. Outside, the churchyard was also full of expectant people. Ricky and Chrissie hadn't advertised their wedding but a heck of a lot of people seemed to have got wind of it anyway. The wedding car drew up and the crowd parted to allow it through. Chrissie with her father, Angela and Joanna Elizabeth, the maids of honour, and Timmy, the page boy, climbed out. The crowd gave a collective *Aaahh!* of delight Angela and Joanna Elizabeth fussed around Chrissie's dress for a moment, then handed her the bouquet. Jason stepped forward and arranged the group pleasingly in the church doorway.

Inside the church Ricky, with Simon at his side, was fidgeting nervously. "Don't worry about it," Simon said. "Everything's in hand."

"Have you got the ring?" Simon rolled his eyes, produced the ring from his pocket, then slid it back again. The vicar leaned forward. "The bride has arrived," he whispered. Ricky looked round but she wasn't there. "Photographs," the vicar whispered. "They'll be a few minutes yet."

Ricky looked across the aisle to where his parents were standing, his mother restraining Baby James, who had just escaped from Chrissie's mother in a moment of inattention. Mrs Epstein smiled apologetically at Mrs Jones, who waved at her cheerfully. The organ struck up the Wedding March and the congregation stood as Chrissie, ethereal in a Joanna Elizabeth original, floated down the aisle.

~* ~

Simon was making his best man's speech to the loud amusement of all their friends.

"And another thing," he said. "Richard is lazy. He married a woman with a ready-made family."

The guests erupted into raucous laughter.

"I told him not to say that," Ricky muttered.

"Oh, don't be such a wet blanket," Chrissie said. "He's doing a great job. I think it's the most interesting best man's speech I've ever listened to. I've learnt all sorts of things about you I didn't know before."

Ricky hid his embarrassment by bending down to talk to Timmy.

Chrissie leaned across. "Did you notice the girl in the red dress?" He had noticed, but had hoped Chrissie hadn't. Tracy in her famous tomato outfit, standing at the edge of the crowd with a face like thunder. "I thought she looked a bit like me," Chrissie said wickedly.

"Good God, no," Ricky said. "Nobody looks like you. You are the one perfect thing in the world," he took her hand under the table and squeezed it tenderly, "Mrs Epstein."

THE END

ABOUT THE AUTHOR

Jenny Twist was born in York and brought up in the West Yorkshire mill town of Heckmondwike, the eldest grandchild of a huge extended family.
She left school at fifteen and went to work in an asbestos factory. After working in various jobs, including bacon-packer and escapologist's assistant (she was The Lovely Tanya), she returned to full-time education and did a BA in history, at Manchester and post-graduate studies at Oxford.
She stayed in Oxford working as a recruitment consultant for many years and it was there that she met and married her husband, Vic.
In 2001 they retired and moved to Southern Spain where they live with their rather eccentric dogs and cat. Besides writing, she enjoys reading, knitting and attempting to do fiendishly difficult logic puzzles. Since moving to Spain she has written four novels and numerous short stories.

In July 2018 she was awarded the coveted TOP FEMALE AUTHOR award in Fantasy/Horror/Paranormal/Science Fiction by The Authors Show

..

Visit Jenny on her Facebook page. She loves talking to her readers.

https://www.facebook.com/pages/Jenny-Twist-Author/291166404240446

Or you can follow her on her website:
https://sites.google.com/site/jennytwistauthor/home

Goodreads Author Page
http://www.goodreads.com/author/show/4848320.Jenny_Twist

Amazon Author Page
US: amazon.com/author/jennytwist
UK: http://www.amazon.co.uk/Jenny-Twist/e/B005CI80ZC/ref=ntt_athr_dp_pel_1If

ACKNOWLEDGEMENTS

I first came across the theory of alternative dimensions from reading John Wyndham. He may even have invented it for all I know. I have a lot to thank John Wyndham for. His stories have given me pleasure throughout my life. I have read them over and over again and still do.

Thanks to Tara Fox Hall for making me write the story in the first place, and to Su Halfwerk, not just for being the best cover designer in the world, but also for being a staunch friend and honest critic. Thanks to Emily Hetherington, my beloved granddaughter, for editing and proofreading.
And thanks to my beta readers, 5 of whom are authors, 3 of whom are (or were) English teachers. I am so fortunate to have them.
Caroline Ritson
Emily Hetherington
Irene Duncan
Janet Doolaege
Julie Devine
Lynette Sofras
Su Halfwerk
Tori Wooldridge
Debbie Black
Mary Patterson Thornburg.
I love you all.

Joanna Elizabeth is a real person and very dear to me. She is the daughter I never had. Presently she is working as a fashion designer in Paris. Today Paris, tomorrow the world!

www.ingramcontent.com/pod-product-compliance
Lightning Source LLC
Chambersburg PA
CBHW071526150726
48000CB00002B/705